THE ELEVEN

by
Kyle Deville

iUniverse, Inc.
New York   Bloomington

iUniverse books may be ordered through booksellers or by contacting:

iUniverse
1663 Liberty Drive
Bloomington, IN 47403
www.iuniverse.com
1-800-Authors (1-800-288-4677)

ISBN: 978-1-4401-1365-9 (sc)
ISBN: 978-1-4401-1368-0 (ebook)

Printed in the United States of America

iUniverse rev. date: 01/06/2009

Something Strange Happened Here

1

She stood at the front of the lawn. It seemed to have been forever that she was standing there. The trip coming to the house was even long. And by the time that she had got out of the car, her legs were numb.

"Shall we go in?" A man asked as he looked over at her. She didn't know him. And she didn't like him either. But he held the keys, and after a few seconds of waiting for her to speak, he started to walk through the lawn and to the front door.

As she was led into the house she could smell the stench of death. It was so strong. And it had made her want to be sick. But she would not be. She would be strong. Stronger than *they* could ever imagine.

2

Her name is Emily Cross. She knew that, even though they had beat her and made her bleed. She had been taken and brought here to this house out in the woods. Away from everything that she knew. Taken away from her friends and family. Away from her boyfriend, with whom she had been seeing for nearly three years. Taken away with a brute force from the parking lot of her work late in the night.

They had waited for her for an hour. Sitting in a van and watching the back door for her to come out. And she did. And *they* had taken her.

Emily had received a phone call earlier that night. She had been told to make it a short one since she was *not* supposed to be receiving personal calls at work.

After she walked out the back door after work, she headed to her Toyota. And it was upon reaching into her purse, and standing next to the drivers side door, that *they* had come from behind her and took her away.

Three men and two women.

One of the men had bear hugged her from behind while the girl placed a white pillow case over Emily's head. Emily *did* catch a glance at the girl and one of the men (not the one who held her tight), she would see him later.

She was placed in the van and driven to a house. She had no idea of where she stood after the ride was over. But she had guessed the ride to have taken a good forty miles to get there.

The house was not very big. And it was not run down. It was very well kept, and in a way picturesque.

When Emily had gotten out of the car, *they* had taken off the pillow case from over her head. *They* had *wanted* her to see.

"Welcome to your new home," the girl said. She was a short haired brunette who wore thick glasses. And she was cute. She had dark brown eyes, and wore a tight pink shirt (short-sleeved), with tight black jeans. And sandals.

Sandals? Why is she going to wear sandals to kidnap someone? Emily had thought as she stood in silence and waited for something to happen. And after a minute or two, something did.

They took her inside.

As soon as Emily stepped inside she was told to take off her shoes. Which she did with no back talk on the matter. Two men were now standing outside. And the one man with whom had bear hugged her had come in with the cute brunnete girl. The other man who was there in the parking lot to help in the assist of her kidnap had disappeared. Emily had only seconds to the thought of that man before the *other* one allowed himself known to her.

Eric was his name. Tall and skinny. Shaved head. He stood next to two girls. Nadine and Charlotte. Nadine was the cute brunnete with thick glasses. Charlotte was a long haired redhead who resembled the *Wendey's* girl. Only on drugs. Her eyes were dark, and it looked as if she hadn't slept in a few days. She was wearing an all black dress. And nothing else.

Emily didn't speak. She just stood by that front door and had a look around. The first thing that she noticed was that there was no furniture. The second was the color of the interior of the house. It was all black inside. The walls, ceiling, steps and railing. Even the carpet was black. And there seemed to be no electricity. For the house was candle lit. All white candles. Placed on the floor, along the bottom of the black walls. Some of the candles were almost burnt out and had burned down and settled into a white pile of wax. And to Emily, that didn't seem to have any concern for the three others who were standing next to her.

Emily could see something as well. Something crawling up the walls. At first she wasn't so sure. Maybe it was the reflections of the candle light. She tried to make it out while Eric and Nadine talked about obtaining something to eat. Charlotte just stood and looked at them, and at her. Her arms were crossed under her breasts, and she looked eager to do something.

Suddenly, Emily jumped as something crawled across her foot. It was a spider. And it goosebumps and a chill over her body. Eric and Nadine had stopped talking and looked at her. Charlotte was looking as well. But, she had already *been* looking.

"They are everywhere," Eric said to Emily as she rubbed her hands over her arms. She was trying to find comfort by hugging herself. She hated spiders. Hated them with a passion. And it was now obvious to her that these three other people (her captors), did *not* have a fear of those spiders themselves.

"Take her upstairs to room number three," Eric told Nadine and Charlotte. They did as they were told and led Emily up the stairs. Nadine held Emily's hand as they went up. She could hear the stairs creak as she ascended each step. And at times, she could feel her feet step on (and crush), some of the spiders. She could feel their juicy insides run out of their hairy bodies as her feet laid into them. She could *hear* the crunch of the bodies. And she wasn't sure, but Emily came to believe that some of the spiders had bit her feet with each step. The top of that staircase did not come soon enough.

Room three was (of course), the third door down the hallway and to the right. Nadine knocked three times on that door and it was opened by a midget wearing a clown outfit. His face was painted black with two red diamonds around his eyes. "Bring her in," he told Nadine and to Charlotte with an emotionless voice. Emily stood quietly between them. She waited to be led into the room, but before they would let her in the two girls gave her a kiss on her right and left cheek. They then stood before her and began to kiss each other. It was long and passionate. And when they were done, and stood on either side of Emily, the midget in the clown outfit looked up at them and asked: "Must you two do that every time?"

The door to room three closed slowly behind her as Emily walked inside.

3

She was told to stand in center of room three. It was dark and candle lit just like the rest of the house. Only in this room, there was furniture. An alter. Hanging above was the rotting head of a goat. Most of the skin had gone away. But what was left was mainly around the eyes and horns. And there was still plenty of dried blood underneath as well as on the places of skull that shown through. There were two candles on either ends of the alter. And a big black book of which sat in center. Beside the book were two daggers with gold handles. And a cup (more so of a grail), made of silver and gold. The gold was a pentegram which pointed south.

Emily heard laughter and looked over and into an open closet door. There, sitting inside, were two more midgets wearing clown outfits. Two women clowns. One had her top down and had what looked to be blood covering her exposed breasts. The other woman midget clown was running her hands over them and licking her small fingers. While the other woman midget clown moaned in pleasure as those little fingers ran across her hard bloody nipples. Both of the woman midget clowns had long black hair and shared the same painted faces as the male midget clown.

"Come and kneel down," the male midget clown told her. He grabbed Emily's hand and led her to the alter. She did as she was told with no hesitation or fuss. The male midget clown stood behind her and raised his arms.

"Oh dark one. With whom your powers I am in want to possess. I offer the blood of this girl. For in return, my dead soul to come alive with the touch of your black kiss."

Emily had never noticed the two women midget clowns come out of the closet. They were kneeling on either side of the alter. And they both held a skull within their own hands. They were human skulls. And Emily didn't was to think of how the midget clown had come about acquiring them. What they had to do. Or where they went. Those thoughts ran in and out of her mind just as fast as she let them come and go. Then there was silence. Nobody spoke for what seemed forever and it made Emily nervous. It was really the first time since being taken from the parking lot that she started to become nervous. Not scared. (At least not yet).

Up till this point in the evening, everything seemed too much like a dream to her. Nothing had seemed real. And Emily kept thinking to herself that at any moment she would wake up in her bed and next to her boyfriend under those cool bed sheets and hot blankets.

That was until the two women midget clowns came over and beside her. One on either side. They grabbed Emily's hands and held her arms up, exposing her wrists to the blackened ceiling. The male midget clown grabbed the dagger from off the alter. He held it in his right hand, blade down. With his left hand, he reached and took hold of the silver cup.

He stood in front of Emily and looked at her with his black eyes. It made her scared. More scared than the fact that she knew she was about to be cut open. So cold and dark his eyes were. So filled with hate.

The male midget clown placed the cup under Emily's right wrist. He then placed the daggers blade against her skin, resting its cold steel on her vein. Then all three of the midget clowns began to chant: "Blood from a girl. Now dead to the world. Blood from a girl. Given to the dark lord."

As the two women midget clowns chanted, and after the blood had filled the silver cup, they each held a skull within their hands high towards the rotting goat head hanging on the blackened wall above the alter. The chant became louder, and the rooms temperature seemed to change in climate.

Outside the air was cool and the moon was bright and full. Dark rain clouds had scattered the dark sky, while bats flew down from between trees that shaded stacks of chicken cages. But there were no chickens caged within. These cages held ducks and rattlesnacks. Side by side with cages sitting directly on top of them. Eight cages all together. Four on the bottom with four on top. Two of the top cages held raw and bloodied meat. Pieces of meat that will *never* become revealed.

The other two cages held spiders. Some were as large as a desert tarantula. And others were small. As small as the ones which are now crawling on the black walls inside the house. The larger spiders are black with blue and white circles covering their black hairy bodies. Their white fangs visible and always ready to bite. These spiders spend their nights crawling wildly over the other. Climbing along the chicken cages. Hungry for the kill.

Blood ran out of Emily's wrist as she sat between the women midget clowns. She felt sick and waited to fade out of this nightmare. She was in pain and loosing too much blood. The cut was made deep. It was sharp and fast. Blood had *squirted* out and over Emily's wrist and hand as well as the male midget clowns as it fell into the silver cup. It was filled half-full. And was then held up and towards the rotting goat head. A spider ran across the black wall and behind the onto the rotting head. It sat still a moment, then crawled underneath the remaining skin.

"For you, my lord," the male midget clown shouted. The two women midget clown giggled at this. The male midget clown turned fast around and gave both women a stern hard look. They silenced themselves quickly and looked down to the blackened floor. The male midget clown turned back and faced the alter again.

In room *one*, Nadine, Charlotte, and Eric laid on the floor together. They had loved each other and were now sharing a bottle of red wine. It was now there second bottle. And the three were nice and buzzed. The girls were on either side of Eric. Nadine on his left. She reached and ran her hand up and down his chest. Charlotte held a glass of the red wine. She finished what was remaining and set the cup next to the almost empty bottle on the floor next to her. She kissed Eric on his neck. Biting and sucking as she moved towards his chest. The night went on.

Emily laid on the floor of room three. She knew that with the amount of blood lost that she could die soon. She was given some wine. Red wine. Given to her from the same cup that at one point held her blood. It was now gone. Shared by those three demonic people after performing the rites to their dark lord. Now they sat together inside that small closet. They stared at Emily and laughed. They looked different to her now. More terrible than before.

Eyes blank. As if there was no one home. As if they were no longer real.

Emily wanted to be sick was too afraid. She was slowly dying. She knew it too fully now, and she was eager to get out and away from this house and get help. She knew there were other houses around. *They* had let her see them.

The three midget clowns began to laugh at her and point. It made Emily angry and if she could she would have hurt them for all that they had done to her. But she knew she couldn't. It would do her no good to even try. But she *would* try to leave. The clowns and this room first. And then down the stairs and out the front door. And then she would run. Run as fast as she could down the long dark street of the neighborhood of which this dark house stood.

Emily slowly got to her hands and knees. And as she did, the clowns laughter became louder. The three of them seemed to have become drunk. With power or wine, Emily would never know. But it became a better chance for her to get away. And so she started to crawl towards the door. The track of blood left would never be seen to the naked eye. But it could be *felt* with the naked foot.

But she crawled. And she did get out. And with not a single bit of trouble from those three midget clowns who sat in a closet within a candle lit room and drank their red wine until they would pass out together shortly after. Light drinkers as the three of them were.

Emily crawled down the hallway. It seemed to her to be so much longer than it had looked before. And she wouldn't know it until it was too late. But she had crawled the wrong way. She had taken a right. When she should have taken a left.

She came to another room. The frame around the door was a bright yellow. It was the only other color in the house that was *not* black.

Probably room four, Emily thought as she looked upon it. *Who gives one?* she thought once more before she opened the door and to crawl inside. Blood ran down her arm as she reached up and grabbed hold of the handle. And it was then that she *knew* she would die here. Her life ended inside this house. But the thought comforted her. She would welcome death. For she would rather die than to spend another night in this hell. Emily opened the door and crawled inside.

And what she saw made her more afraid than anything she had already seen. The room was all yellow. Much brighter than the rest of the house. Which in turn made the situation worse. There was a man sitting in a brown recliner. Empty wine bottles were set next to the chair on a yellow floor. And what was more disturbing was a mannequin which was hung upside-down, and across from the man sitting in the recliner.

It was a woman mannequin. Painted on her stomach was a crucifix which pointed south. Painted on with red paint. On the floor beneath, and surrounding the mannequin, were busted wine bottles. Streaks of red wine ran down the wall. These bottles thrown in a drunken rage by this man who sat in his brown recliner.

The man turned his head and looked at Emily.

"My name is Lucifer Cane. And you are Emily," he tells her with a voice that was dead and yet seemed to echo and rattle the walls of this yellow room.

He looked back at the mannequin. He picked up a bottle of wine and took a long sip. Then, with all his strength, Lucifer Cane threw the bottle . Hurling the bottle at an incredible speed that scared Emily terribly. She shrieked as the bottle hit the wall. Shattering into a million pieces.

"Whore!" Lucifer Cane yelled. His voice was a horrible sound. It was *not* human. And Emily closed her eyes, and covered her ears at the sound of it.

She felt more blood run down her arm. And she felt her stomach begin to turn again. This man, Lucifer Cane, looked upon her with eyes that seemed to burn, and began to laugh. And as he did, Emily rolled onto her back and looked up at a yellow ceiling that was spinning. She looked away at the man named Lucifer Cane and saw that he was *not* really a man at all. He was sort of animal. Half human and half wolf. And he was dead. She could see it clearly now. His own body was rotted and old. And the smell of death came from him as well. Emily began to scream. Then all went black.

4

She awoke on the basement floor. She was cold and all was dark. And just as the rest of the house (and if she could *see* it), the walls and cold cement floor was painted black. She was dizzy. And her head ached terribly from behind her left ear.

Emily reached a hand back to feel behind her left ear and felt something wet from where her pain came from. She ran her fingers over the wet spot and tried to see if it was blood. But the basement room was too dark. She didn't know what to do. She thought that maybe she had been drugged. (In fact, she was one hundred percent sure that she had *not?* been). But she liked the idea anyway. It was a lot better than knowing that someone had knocked her silly from behind. *At least you don't loose any blood when your drugged*, she thought to herself while lying on that cold cement floor.

Emily then remembered that her wrist had been cut open by that demonic male midget clown. She grabbed at her wrist and was relieved to find that her wounded wrist was now bandaged.

"Hello?" Emily cries out with a raspy, sore throat. "Somebody. Anybody." She was starting to become scared again. She hated the dark. And being alone. So she tried again to call for someone. Waiting for anyone, or *anything*, to respond.

"Hello? Someone. If anyone can hear me, then please *answer* me." She was starting to cry now. She so desperately wanted to be heard. To be answered. And someone did.

Lucifer Cane. He was standing on the other side of the basement door. And with light coming from behind it, Emily could see where, and how big, the door was. This man, Lucifer Cane, began to tap on the door lightly. He called to her from behind the shaded door. Called to her with his dead voice that echoed and rattled the shaded door and walls. And laughed ever so lightly as he did so.

"Emily," he called quietly down to her. "Hey, Emily, do you like spiders?" He waited for an answer, and when there was none, he asked again. "I say, do you like spiders?"

"No," Emily answered through her tears. "I hate them."

"Then you will really hate this."

There was a click sound, and the basement light came on, and Emily could see. Only, at this moment, she really wished that she *couldn't*. Now, she wished for the dark. For it to come back. She never thought that the dark could be so good.

Emily hated spiders. Hated them with a cold passion. And now that the basement was lighted, she was now faced with a terrifying truth. She was surrounded by them. Hundreds. Large, hairy, and wet. They crawled up the walls and over the basement floor. There were thick webbing in all four corners. Homes to millions of deadly more of those dark killers.

She *had* been drugged. For if she hadn't been, then she would have felt all of the spiders crawling over her body. And they *were* all over her. Even under her clothes. She could feel two of them crawling under her shirt. They moved slowly, and as they did, Emily could feel their long fangs run along her skin. Knowing that at any second they could sink into her.

One spider, not as big as the others, crawled up the side of her neck. Emily winced as its hairy, wet body ran up to her throat. Its legs digging deep into her skin. Emily was beginning to loose control. She wanted to scream. She *needed* to scream. But then the pain hit her. It was on her foot. She *had* been wearing shoes when she was abducted. But now, as she has painfully discovered, her feet were bare.

It was a bite. She knew it as soon as it happened. And she let herself go. Her emotions. Her sanity. She screamed. So loud that it hurt her own ears. She swung her arms frantically. Throwing off spiders as she did. And being bit as well. She was bit on her stomach. Her back, and the sides of her back. Emily punched at each bite. Punched until there became too many bites. Too much pain. She was covered by those wet, hairy killers. She screamed one last time. And as she did, one spider ran into her open mouth and bit down hard on her tongue.

Emily..... .

5

Stood at the foot of the yard next to her husband. They had driven nearly four hours and were tired as well as very hungry. The two of them didn't want to go into the house, but the real-estate agent had insisted that they get as much of the paperwork done today while they all had the chance.

The real-estate agents name was Nadine. She wore thick black glasses that reminded Emily of Thelma from the *Scooby Doo* cartoons. Her husband Eric held her hand and asked if she was ready to go take a look inside. Both Eric and Nadine waited for Emily's answer. But none came. Nadine finally asked if Emily was feeling alright. She told Eric that his wife looked a little pale and tired. Still with no answer, Eric then asked.

"What is it, Emily? What's wrong?"

"Maybe we could do this tomorrow. If its best for the two of you, that is?" Nadine asked. "I can meet you here by nine tomorrow morning," Nadine told them and looked down at her watch. Then at the house.

Emily continued to stare at the house absently. It made both Nadine and Eric nervous.

Eric broke the silence by saying: "Yes. I think that might be... ."

Emily interrupted him by breaking out of her spell and asking Nadine something with which she would never forget. And because she would never forget was because this was the first day that the recently newly wed couple would have seen their new home. Nadine had *not* shown either of the two any pictures of the interior of the house. Only the exterior. The front, sides, and back. The front and backyard.

"Are the walls black?" Emily asked.

"Yes. But that is one of the things that I had wanted to talk to you both about. Before you two move in, I will send a crew and have the entire interior of the house repainted with the color of your choice. At no extra cost. Of course," Nadine tells them, but is only *half* promising the deal.

"How did you know that the walls were black? If you don't mind me asking you, Mrs. Cross?"

"Yeah. How *did* you know that honey?" Eric asked her as well.

Emily looked away from them both and said: "Something strange happened here."

Within Her Eyes

1

The day she saw me was dancing in an open field with that warm sunlight bearing down upon her face. Her long dirty blonds hair fell all around her shoulders. Her white dress was hidden the dozens of flowers that stood around her. She was beautiful. And from the first time that I saw her I knew that I wanted to be with her.

She is so free and different. And she seemed to dance to the sound of music that could only be heard by her alone. By her own ears. I wanted to approach her. But then he appeared. Her man. Or at least, her man for the moment.

He held her hands and kissed her on her full red lips. I had to sit back against some tree and watch. I hated it. Seeing her with him made me sick in my stomach. And it brought an incredible rage from inside me. They hugged. And as they did, she looked at me. I sat nest to that tree and felt my heart stop. She had caught me staring. And now it was too late to look away. Now she would know. My crush for her was discovered. Out for her eyes to see. And if I could have the opportunity to just tell her how I felt for her. To tell her just how beautiful I think she really was. If only she could know.

Of course I know. I have always *known.*

Wait. Did that just happen? Did she just speak to me? She is *still* looking at me. So what does that mean?

Yes. I am speaking to you. Her voice again. Only, I am the only one who can hear it. Telepathy. Is that what is going on here? So I ask her how she had known. Only I didn't use my mouth. Just my mind.

She was still holding onto her boyfriend looking at me with those dark eyes of hers. She then responds and I fell a jolt of pain as I received her answer . Not bad. But just enough to close my eyes as it ran through my mind.

It doesn't matter how *I know. Just that I* do *know. I know when you look at me. And I know what you think and feel for me.*

And then she smiled. And so I smiled back. And I felt a warmth run through my heart that I had never felt before. And then it was over. And she was gone and away from me again. I sat under that tree and watched her walk away with this guy when it should have been me. I wondered when when I might see her again.

Soon. Very soon, I heard her say. And she looked back one more time at me with those dark eyes. Her arm around the waist of the man that she was with. But there was something there. Something that I had not picked up on before. I only felt it for a brief moment. And when

I did, her eyes were darker. And that warmth that I had felt before turned cold and full of pain. And death.

Her eyes told me something. Only, I did not know what it was.

But you will soon find out, she said to me as she looked at me. Then she looked away from me. But before she did, I once again felt that warmth from her run through my mind and my heart. The pain and death was forgotten. And so was she.

I sat there in at the edge of that field and watched the sun go down before going home.

2

My name is Brian. I am twenty eight, single, and I am going to tell you a story. A story about a girl named Elizabeth. The day that I finally saw her again was shortly after I started my third year of college. I was taking classes for a business major and had happened to see her on my way to class one cold afternoon. It was mid November now, (about a month since the day that we saw each other at that open field), and I had just turned the corner from the girls dorm. It was on the way, and quite unavoidable to pass by. But what guy would want to pass it by. Right?

And there she was. Standing with some other girls and holding some books of her own. She was wearing a black sweater and blue jeans. Her hair was twice as long as it was before. And it was done up in these curls. As I passed by, we looked at each other. She watched me as I walked by without a single blink of an eye. And I couldn't look away. Not even if some madman started to scream and wave a gun. I wouldn't look away. But I gotta tell you, that if even *you* saw her, then you would be put within her spell as well.

She watched me walk by and even to the building for my class. I know this because before I walked inside I looked back to her and saw that she was still looking right at me. Right into my eyes and down into my heart. I felt a chill run over my body. And till this day, I cannot tell if it was from the cold wind that had picked up at that moment, or the long look coming from Elizabeths dark eyes.

We stood at our places for those few seconds in time until I was pushed out of the way by a student in some kind of hurry. I didn't see Elizabeth again until a week later, downtown at a bar, with some friends of hers while I was with some of mine.

I had downed a few beers and had a shot of whiskey when I saw her. She was with the same friends that I had seen her with that afternoon. They were sitting at a table. And she had one of them call me and my buddies over to join them. They had been watching us for some time.

Elizabeth sat in a corner with her friends Heather, Shirley, and Katherine. I sat there with my buddies Stan and William. They all talked and drank up a storm. While Elizabeth and I listened and looked each other over. We spoke to each other with our eyes. And at times would even laugh. Our friends looked at the two of us as if we were mad. Elizabeth and I would just shrug it off and would go back to our little game.

I had awoke the next morning with a light hangover. But it was easy to care for since all I thought about was *her*. We did have a moment together outside the bar before everyone left for the evening.

"It was really nice to have finally met you, Elizabeth," I said to her as I looked into those dark eyes. She took my hand, which were oddly cold, and said:

"Please, call me Liz. Okay?" she said to me with the sweetest voice.

"Okay. Sure," I said back to her. There was a moment of silence as we looked at each other and then she smiled. She has the nicest smile. Full lips and dimples. Her long hair almost hid her face. A cool breeze had picked up as we looked at each other. Our friends were dancing around us while laughing and talking about god knows what. And then it was over.

Her friends had said that it was time to go. And she did. She looked at me and waited for me to say something, but I just stood there. I didn't want to look as if I *needed* her. And I didn't want to say anything that would make me show how deep my feelings for her had become. And so I just stood there and watched her leave. Something that I would do quite a lot in the coming weeks after that night.

I would see her sometimes during school hours. And she would see me. But no matter who she was with, she would always smile. And I would smile back. And that would be it.

But there was also those times when I would get a glimpse of something from the corner of my eye. A darkness. A darkness that seemed void. Empty. And when I would look, there she would be. Standibng alone. In fact, those were the few times that I did see her alone.

And those were the few times that I would get nervous. Only, I couldn't understand as to why.

There was no smile from either one of us during those moments. And thankfully, those moments didn't happen often. But what I do remember the most was how she would look at me. A look that I still cannot figure. It is strange. And I know that sounds bleak. But that was what it was. It was as if she was someone else. A whole other person. Older. And yet, not old at all.

This went on for nearly a month. I knew that she was involved. And so I had stayed a safe distance from her. Waiting for the right moment to make my move. But I didn't want ot date her. I wanted to *know* her. I wanted our sould to touch. As will happen from time to time. I had wanted it. And I got it. Got it real good.

I was sitting on my couch when I had gotten the phone call from my mother telling me about everyone who was going to be home for the Christmas holiday. And I assured her, (more than I needed to), that I would be home for the holiday.

I fell asleep shortly after hanging up the phone. The conversation had taken a lot out of me. And I slept good and long. Nearly eleven hours. I awoke around ten the next morning feeling ready to take on the rest of the day. Exam week would be coming up, and I had a lot of studying to do.

3

I had driven home for that Christmas. It took just under four hours to get there. And believe me when I tell you that I was more than happy to open that front door and see everyone there. Especially the beer and food. Which I had plenty of.

I had welcomed that break with open arms. Exam week had been hard. And it was nice to get away for a while. But I still had Elizabith, (Liz), in the back of my mind. I thought of her when I fell asleep. And she was the first thing on my mind when I woke up.

I didn't get much as far as gifts go. I had told my parents that I didn't want anything. Let alone *need*. But I do that anyway. And for the first time they had listened. What I did get were some books, and lot of food and alcohol. All were much appreciated.

When I got back to my dorm the weekend before school break was to be over, I took a rather long walk. Just something that I do from time to time. I walked for nearly an hour. And as much as I tried, I could not steer my thoughts away from her. At it was at that moment that I realized, that Liz had become somewhat of an obsession for me. I wanted her so much that it hurt to have those feelings. And what hurt more was that I didn't know when, (or if), I would ever see her again.

After my walk I laid on my bed and watched some T.V. I cant remember what I watched. But I don't think that it really matters. I fell asleep shortly and had awoken later that night. So I took another long walk. The night air was cold. And my hands were numb even inside my pockets. My throat hurt, while the moon shined bright in that dark sky. And there was no sound. Just me and the night. I really didn't want it to end.

It was quarter to two that early morning when I got back to my dorm room. And upon entering, I noticed the answering machines light blinking. So I, (of course), checked to see what the message was. And what I heard was almost nothing. *Almost* nothing. Because there was slience up until the end. A choking sound before the message ended.

I played it again. Only this time with the sound turned up. And this time when I listened, I could hear someone breathing, and the sound of someone whispering in the background. I do not knoe till this day what that person was whispering. And truth be told, I don't want to know. It all sounded wrong. And as I stood there after the message had played through the second time, I had the feeling that I was being watched. Watched by someone outside in the cold dark night looking in and watching me.

Then I finished the school year. And then the next. And then I graduated. And one night shortly after graduation I realized that, (even thought I still had thoughts about Liz and *would* at timed see her around campus), I really *hadn't* seen her since that one night so long ago at the bar.

So I made myself forget. I had to. I couldn't imagine it being too healthy thinking about one person all the time. And so I forgot about her. I worked. All days. And at night I would spend time with my friends. I dated whenever I could. I, simply put, tried to live a simple life.

I just worked, saved my money, and forgot all about her. And it worked. Until I was sitting in a coffee shop one afternoon, reading a book, when I heard a couple talking and happened to look up and see Liz. She came over to me immediately when she saw me looking up at her.

"How have you been?" Liz asked me. She was holding some books of her own that she held against her stomach. She was just as beautiful as she was the last time that I had sen her.

"I'm doing alright, Liz," I told her and smiled. There was a moment of silence between that two of us as we looked at each other. "Would you like a seat?" I asked her. She didn't answer. And there was more silence to be had. So I said: "I think your friend is waiting for you."

Liz turned and looked. Then she looked back at me and told me she would be right back. Which she did in a matter of seconds.

"That was Anne," Liz says as she sits down next to me. "I work with her at the office, although she doesn't put in as many hours as I do." She placed her books down on the table. I was about to ask her what she was carrying when she turned them slightly so I could see.

She had four books. One was about religion. Two on relationships and finding love. And the fourth was about a serial killer. A guy named Richard... . I cannot remember the last name at the moment. But the media had called him *The Night Stalker*.

4

It was on a Wednesday night that Liz and I started to see each other. And that was also the night that we got *close*. We had met up at a bar.I was not entirely in the mood for a drink, but knowing that Liz was there waiting for me? Well, lets just say that I would have tried every drink there if she had asked me too.

"So, where are you from?" I ask her.

"Originally from Penn. State, but I now live over in Hampton Hills."

I know all about that place. A very nice apartment complex that overlooks a park at the bottom of this massive hill. Its not too far from where I live. I cant imagine what the rent is.

"I should have you over sometime. If you like?" Liz says and smiles. She held my hand, and I held hers back. Cold. Just like that night long ago while the two of us stood outside that bar while saying our goodbyes. I tried to ignore it and looked into her dark eyes. So lovely and inviting they were.

We had a few drinks. The music played loud and good. The place got crowded. We each saw some friends of our owen. It was a good night. One of those nights that you just never wanted to end.

We took a walk later. Around the downtown area. The scene was beautiful Bright lights and warm weather. Other couples walked by us deeply in love. It made the two of us happy to see it. It had seemed that seeing others happy made useven happier. Closer.

At the end of the date, we stood next to her car. She, leaning against her car door while I, was held my hands around her waist. That kiss was the best I have ever had.

"I hope you like me. Because I like you," Liz whispered in my ear. "I like you so much that I am *loving* you."

"Well," I said, "don't stop." Then we kissed again. Long and passionately. Out hands explored each other body. I ran my fimgers through Liz's long dirty blonde hair. Cars drove by, and I know that people were watching us. But I didn't care. And I know that Liz didn't either.

"Goodnight, my love," Liz said to me.

"Goodnight to you my darling," I said to her. We gave each other a hug and she got in her car. I shut the door for her. And that was when things got weird. As Liz started the car up, the windows *clouded*. Not too bad. But just enough so that the corners of all the windows *iced* over. I thought that maybe she had the A/C on. But that wouldn't have made any since. The weather wasn't that hot yet. And so the only thing that I could do was knock on the window. She never noticed. And as cold as it had to have been inside that car, I never saw breath run out as usually happens in colder climates.

Then she pulled out of the parking space and drove off. She never waved goodbye. And she drove away a little too fast for someone driving out of a public parking lot.

We met again that Saturday. We had another round of drinks at the same bar. She wore black jeans and a tight black sweater. Accompanied by black leather boots. Somewhat gothic. But still very nice. It made her more beautiful than she already was.

We stayed for an hour then went to my place. Having Liz stay with me that night was something that I will never forget. It was the best experience that I have had to date. Every touch of her smooth skin made me feel as though I was *falling* into her. I *was* falling into her. And I never wanted to get out.

I awoke later that night after I thought that I had burned myself. My hand. I immediately awoke from my dream, (although I don't know *what* I was dreaming now), and held my hand. Yes I had burned myself. Somewhere in my sleep I had placed my hand on Liz's back. Which I now did awake and felt that same screaming pain from the heat of her body run through my skin. She wasn't hot. She was torching. As hot as an oven turned up to the highest temperature.

"Whats wrong?" Liz asked me without turning over to look at me. Her voice, somewhat sounding sarcastic within her question, made me want to yell. My hand hurt and I was very tired and was in no mood for any wise-ass remarks.

Nothing," I said to her. "Go back to sleep."

"Okay. I love you," she said.

"I love you, too," I told her. And I did. For a little while.

I fell asleep shortly after. Only this time, I kept my back to hers and held the blankets tightly over my body so as to not touch into hers. She was half the time cold. And now she was hot. I didn't know what to think then, and still don't know.

Things went on for the two of us. And within a few weeks, we were an actual couple. And when I say things went on for us, I mean they *really* went on. We even took time to take off for a week together. And in all that time,

I never stepped foot into Liz's apartment. And it was then that I decided to stop by for a friendly visit.

It happened on another Wednesday night. And the time was much later than I had intended. The parking lot was full of cars. But not a single person was in sight. Her apartment was on the third floor of a four story building. A rather dark building I noticed as I walked to the outside staircase. It was almost as if the building was vacant. And I would have believed it if it wasn't for the lights coming from some of the apartment windows.

Liz lived in apartment 1056B. I stood outside her apartment a minute before knocking on the door. And after I did, there was no answer. I checked if the door was locked. It wasn't. So I stood there another minute before going inside.

She was not home. But by the looks of the apartment, I had wondered if I had even walked into the *right* one. It was dark. Cold. And there was mold running up the walls from the floor and up. And there was a smell. The smell of death.

The first place that I looked at was her bedroom. There was no bed, or dressers. In fact, there was no *anything*. Not in this room, or any other part of the apartment. And so I decided to leave. And I did. But as I made my way through the apartment and to the fromt door, there was that darkness from the corner of my eye. Just like all those other times. And so I looked, but this time I didn't see Liz standing there. I didn't see anything at all. Just an empty apartment.

My nerves were starting up, and so I left just as fast as I could. And it wasn't until I had driven a good one, two miles, that I started to feel normal again.

As soon as I had gotten home and into bed, my phone began ringing. At first I didn't want to answer it. But then I thought about how I had not heard (or seen), Liz all day. And so I answered the phone.

"Hello?" I asked. (I now remember that my apartment seemed a bit too cool for me as I stood there with the phone against my ear.

"Next," a deep voiced answered.

"What? Who is this?" I asked. That voice. It was not of a man or of a woman. And it was truly strange to hear.

"Your next," that deep voice said to me.

"I don't know who this is, and I don't care much for you calling me at this hour, so I'm going to hang up," I said. But before I could say my final farewell, that voice turned into a high pitched scream and warned me to: "STAY OUT OF HERE!"

I know what the voice was talking about. It was Liz's apartment. But it didn't make a lick of since. There was nothing in that apartment. *Nothing*.

Our relationship became a little strained after that night. I saw her less and less. More phone calls than actual appearances. We would make plans to meet. But she would never show up.

But then I finally saw her. Two weeks after that night in her apartment and after that call. I was awoken from a chill. The blankets were still covering my body, but I felt that chill none-the-less.

I turned over onto my side and looked at the time. The clock said 3:47 a.m. I laid onto my back and rubbed at my eyes. And as I did I had that feeling *again* that I was being watched. *Knew* that I was being watched.

I didn't want to look, but I made myself do it anyway. And I was right. I was being watched. I looked out my bedroom window and saw Liz standing there, staring right at me with those dark eyes. She didn't look *right*. What I mean is, she didn't look *alive*. Her skin was so pale that it held a light blue. Her lips were more purple in color, than that lovely red.

She looked into my eyes was such hate that I couldn't even move. And I felt something. That same something that I had felt before. I became dizzy and light headed. And I felt colder than I already had. My heart seemed to pound with every beat. I thought I was dying myself. And I was. She was killing me. Killing me with some power within her eyes. And I could see things. I could see other men that she had killed. And *how* she had killed them. And what she had done to their bodies. (Something that will *not* be told). And I could see where those men were now. Even *after* death.

"Let me in," she told me with her mind. "Let me in NOW! I only came over to spend the night with you." She smiled, and tried to become that girl with whom had captured my heart. She was beautiful again. I don't know *how* she did it. But she did. She was *alive*. And so beautiful. She ran her fingers through that long dirty blonde hair. From her hair down and over her breasts. All those horrible feelings, and images, were gone. Almost forgotten.

"Please let me in. I am cold and I want you to hold me till I'm warm again," Liz tells me and looks as though she wants to cry.

"You need to go," I told her in return. I wanted to keep this as short as possible. Just having to tell Liz (a girl who is so gorgeous), to leave was one of the hardest things that I have ever done. But I did it anyway.

"I want us to be close again," she said. "Don't you remember how in love we were? I want that again. And I know that you do too."

I just looked at her. And I almost *did* let her in. And not just in my apartment. I almost let her in my *heart*. I began to remember. All those good times that we shared. And all the love. Yes. I almost let her in again.

But then it happened. Liz became angry with me. And those images, and that cold horrid feeling came rushing bak at me. And she started to speak to me agin. With both her mouth and mind.

"I care so much about you,"

I am going to get you yet... .

"I just want to spend my life with you and love you,"

Just let me in and I will help you forget all about the pain. You won't hurt like the others because I... .

"care so much about you and... ."

"I want you to go, Elizabeth. And I think it best that you not come back," I told her. But not with my mouth, but my mind.

Liz backed away from the window with such rage within her eyes that I looked away. And I would not look back. Not even when she told me (which were the last words that she ever said to me), before walkng away, that: "You will be sorry for this."

And yeah. Maybe I am sorry. Maybe I should have taken her back in. Into my heart and life. At least there would be more memories. (That's if I made it out alive).

Or maybe I should have let her in and had that one last night of *love* before I died.

When your with someone, there is always the talk of what *could* be. And a lot of the time, that is where problems arise. I try my best not to do that. I would much rather be happy with what I have, when I have it. But in this case, I have no idea *what* I had. And maybe it best that I don't know.

It hurts. When I felt about the pain of loosing her. Walking away from her. And I never want to go through that again. And I won't. I will not go back. Even as I write this to you, I will not go back. Because even now, as I sit under this tree at the foot of this open field on another sunny afternoon, she is with me. I can see that darkness from the corner of my eye again. She is watching me. And waiting. But I will not go. No matter what she says. And no matter how beautiful she appears to be. I will not go.

Alone In The Dirt

1

Lying in wait. But what is it that he is waiting for? He knows that this is no lomger a dream. He knows, because evry once in a while, he will awake to the voice of that place that calls to him. And to everyone else who ends up here.

It is that place where you fall deep into. It is an abyss. A black and cold place where you become lost within the darkness. Lost within, when you tire of being here. *Here*, in the absence of the living. *Here*, alone with nothing but your memories and thoughts. *Here*, alone in the dirt.

2

Jeffery McDaniels was buried on a Saturday afternoon in early spring. As his family and friends stood around his coffin and cried, Jeffery lay inside and tried his best to make his scream heard. He screamed so loud that he could feel his throat tear open and feel the pain run down and into his cold lungs.

He had become sick through mid-winter. It had started as a bad cold and developed into pneumonia. He was placed in the hospital to recover after collapsing on the living room floor. What Jeffery remembered when he awoke on that hospital bed, was a strong dizziness, before the world went black.

He had died two weeks later. And now he is lying in his coffin and looking up at his family and friends as they stand around his black box, crying. He *still* at times will believe that this is all a dream. But that will fade away as soon as that black coffin will lower and he sees the dark muddy walls rise around him.

It was weeks and weeks with mothing but his thoughts and memories, and the constant sound of the living, to haunt *him*. He couldn't believe it. The *haunting* of the dead. He never thought it possible while he was living. But it was true. The dead *is* haunted. Haunted by the undying realization that they can never go back to the land of the living. And that they are haunted by the images, and the *sounds* of their family, friends, and lovers. The dead watch as those people move on without them. Watching move on into their new lives. A life without *them*.

Some of the dead accept this fact easily. And some cannot. And those are the ones who fall as fast as they can into that black abyss. Falling deep within, without thought to their new conscious mind. That new conciousness that is awoken upon the body dying.

And now a month has gone by. And sometimes Jeffery likes to think that maybe he was buried alive. He lays and thinks that maybe *they* had made a mistake. That those doctors that looked over him maybe *thought* that he was dead. When he was only sleeping.

But that's not even possible. They *don't make those types of mistakes. Do they? Think about it Jeff, how many times were you checked that week while you were on that bed in that white, cold room? Trying your best to rid yourself from that nasty pneumonia.*

Not very many.

Maybe you were murdered. Those doctors and nurses never wanted you there to begin with. And besides, how many times did she *come to see you? One time. The entire week.*

Stop it! I don't want to think about it.

She had come by to see you the first night that you were there. And then the next day, she had gone to see him. *That other boy. She had gone to see him because she was too upset over the news of your failing health. She* knew *that you were not going to make it to see the end of the week. She knew just like your mother and father.*

Pleas stop. I don't want anymore. So just STOP!

But I can't. And it is time that you face the truth. No matter how painful it may be. Did you know that on their second night together they touched *each other? You had to have known that. They touched each other for nearly an hour. But you* should *be pleased to know that even though she was with another man, she still thought about you while he was inside her.*

I told you to stop. I don't want to hear anymore. Get me out of this. Out of this box. I WANT OUT! OH PLEASE GOD LET ME OUT!

But he cannot get out. And he was reminded again of that painful truth by that voice. That voice that talks to him. At times distant. And at times close. Jeffery did not know where (or even *how*), the voice came to him. It just did. And always at the right time. Those times when Jeffery could go mad. And what a ridiculous idea *that* is. The dead going mad?

Maybe you should see a shrink, Jeffery.

Leave me alone, why don't you. Unless you want to help. Just let me out of here. I want to go back.

But you can't go back. Nobody can. When you get here, you stay here. That is until you decide to leave and come to me. But as far as going back to the living, never. Your time is up there.

3

More time alone. And more time to hear and see the visions of what *was* his life. And more time to get used to the small space that he is now enclosed in. He had estimated over and over that he had a good three to four inches of space from where his rotting body lay, to the black wooden box that he must *now* call home. And yes, his body rotted. And he watched it all. But luckily for him, he could not feel (or smell), the dacay.

Month after month. And year after year, Jeffery lay in his new home and watched while listening as like outside the box moved on without him. He watched his family grow and move on. He watched as his former lover and friends grew and moved on. He watched until he could take it no longer.

How many years had it been? He didn't even want to know. He wanted to *move* on himself, but was scared. He did not know as to what awaited him beyond in the darkness. That abyss that spoke to him every so often. Just a friendly reminder to let him know that *it* was there.

I'm ready. Take me away from this lonely place. I no longer want it.

Okay. That voice again. There without a second of hesitation. *Then say goodbye to the world of the living, Jeffery. And say hello to the darkness. I have waited a long time for you. But I* will *wait longer if need be.*

No. I am ready NOW!

And with those words spoken to the great abyss, Jeffery McDaniels soul was taken from that dark and muddy place and looked upon the enormous black pit. He could feel the tug coming from within that darkness.

Welcome, the abyss said to him.

Jeffery fell. Deep into the darkness. And as he did, he saw that there was no end to this darkness. It was eternal just as death.

Where am I going?

Only time will tell that, Jeffery. And you have all the time in the universe to find out.

And with that, the soul of Jeffery McDaniels fell deep into the abyss. Within his coffin, all that remained were a few remaining pieces of bones. Broken. Dusty. And dark in color.

Valentines Day

1

The morning was cold. And the sky was red as the sun began to rise. It was dark. The color of blood. But faded with the coming morning light.

The day had started normal enough for the city of Fredericksburg. It was a Wednesday, and thigs were going on just as usual as yesterdayn and the days before that. The early birds got up early. The students got up (though not with much of a happy heart), while their mothers made breakfast for them. The fathers read the morning papers and drank their coffee before headinf off to the office.

Yes, it looked to be a rather good day. There was not a cloud in the sky. And it was also a holiday. Today is Valentines Day.

It is a holiday where you are either really excited to get it. Or you would rather jump off a bridge, or take a few pills to numb the pain of being the only person on the entire planet who doesn't have that special someone to share it with. But not on this day. This day *everyone* will have their valentine. Whether they like it. Or not.

2

Heather was dressed and ready before her two younger sisters, Casey and Samantha. She waited by the front door for them. After waiting a while, Heather decided to warm up the car. Unlike herself, Casey and Samantha were not what you would call *morning people*.

Her car started without a hint of problem. Which was good since she had just spent well over three hundred to have it fixed. So there was no problem there. But a problem no less. Sitting on the front passenger seat were two roses and a note. Dirt covered the edges of the torn piece of paper. *Wet* dirt. Like good soil. The note was written with red ink. Heather thought that kinda cute, being that it was Valentines Day. She picked up the note and read:

> *Heather,*
>
> *May this day bless us with the blood of our love.*
>
> *Forever Yours,*
>
> *Jeffery*

Heather sat in her car and felt fear run through her. Her heart nearly stopped when upon reading the name at the end of that note.

Jeffery. My old boyfriend. My... .

Tears began to fill her eyes. And her lips trembled. Jeffery and Heather had dated for three years. She was then a young seventeen. And he nineteen. It was his last year of high school, as she was in her second. Jeffery had died that year running his car off the road after a party with some of his buddies. Heather had asked him not to go out that night. But he had regardless. He had ended up on a hospital bed in a coma. Only to die a day later. It was early on a Sunday morning when it had happened. Heather was with her family attending service when he passed away.

She had attended his funeral with her mother by her side. She had held her tears until they left that day and were heading home. She had been angry with him. But she missed him more than anything. *Still* does.

She had it bad for a while after his untimely passing. But with time she got better. And even though she is alright now, Jeffery is never far from her thoughts. No matter how hard she tries to let him go.

And now she sits in her car with a note that is claiming to be from her deceased boyfriend. And the red ink. Too dark and *wet*.

This isn't ink at all. It's blood. His *blood.*

Heather screamed and ran out of the car and into the house. She was not only upset, she was enraged.

Four blocks away, Jim sat in his chair on his front porch and drank his morning coffee. It was just one of the things that he used to do with his Wife Emma before she had passed away herself a week after last Christmas. She had a stroke. At fifty seven, Emma was what all thought to be in great shape. But who would ever guess, right?

He hurt all the time. And at timed Jim thought that he could hear her calling his name. How he missed her so.

He had made an appointment to see about receiving meds for his migraines. He had been having them since Emma's passing. Sometimes they hurt so bad that he couldn't see straight. He started to think about her again and tears fell from his eyes.

No. Don't do this old man. Not today. It don't even matter that its Valentines Day. Emma and you never even cared for that stupid holiday anyway. So, lets not do this now. Deal? This is not something that she would have wanted to see you do. Think of her smile. Think of that thick hair. Think... .

SLAM!

That front door had shut so hard that Jim jumped to his feet, spilling half of his coffee. He stood for a minute and looked around. He placed his cup of coffe down on the little table that stood between his chair and Emma's. He had spilled his cup of Joe over his pants, shirt, and hand. It had burned like hell when it hit his skin. But now it just felt *sticky*.

All he saw was a few cars drive by, and some students making there way to class at the university. He may have been on the porch alone, but would he be alone inside as well?

He looked into the living room window. He was expecting to see someone, but all he saw was the same old furniture with the same old television set. More cars drove by, and more students walked on towards campus. And he was glad for it. The sounds of those cars and voices helped him to get his nerves back. He was scaring himself.

Just the wind old man. Nothing more.

But there had been no wind. Because if there was, then he sure as hell would *not* have been sitting outside drinking his coffee. Which he then remembered that he still had. A good half cup left, cooling on the outside table. Jim picked up his cup, took a sip, and went inside.

"If this is someone's idea of a joke, then you can all go to HELL!" Heather screamed at her sisters. Her parents stood and waited for the yelling from all three of their children to stop before stepping in. Heather ran into the kitchen (with Casey and Samantha hot behind her trail), and threw the two roses and note into the trash.

"We didn't do anything to you, Heather," Casey yelled, "so stop giving us this bullshit!"

"Casey, that's enough!" the girls mother yelled. "I have had it with the three of you. It is too early for this and... ."

Heather decided that she did not want to hear a lecture and stormed out of the kitchen and house. But before she walked out that front door, she had one more thing to say to her younger sisters: "Hurry the hell up!"

A minute later, Casey, Samantha, and their mother came outside together. Heather was asked to get out of the car (which she did as Casey and Samantha got in), and talk to her mother for a minute.

"I will drive them to school. When I get back we will talk about this, okay?"

"Sure. Whatever," Heather says softly. Her face was red from crying. And her heart was pounding.

"Please calm down. Your sisters did not put those roses, or that note in your car. And I think you know that. Don't you?"

"Well, they had better not have. Because that would be some really sick shit if they did, and utterly disgusting."

"Please don't use that language. And please don't fight with her sisters. Or me," her mother says and run her fingers through Heathers hair. It had always calmed her when she was upset. Casey and Samantha just sat in the car and waited. They only had ten minutes to get to school now.

Heather gave her mother a hug and walked up the the front door. She turned as her mother drove her sisters to school. Then she paid her attention to the yard across the street. There was a line of bushes that was used as their neighbors gate. You see, when Heather had hugged her mother, she saw a boy standing behind that row of bushes. He was wearing a black suit with no shoes. He had *grey* eyes and pale skin. She had only looked for a second before turning back to her mother and walking back to the house.

This time when she looked, the boy was gone. Heather looked both ways on her block but saw nothing new. She decided to forget about it and went to bed.

John was a carpenter who had taken a job repairing the ceiling to the store-room to the Catholic church. The store-room was set above the massive organ that sat all around the alter. There were speakers that were placed below what looked like air vents. Air vents made of wood. Set up on high and looking down above the entire church floor.

Behind these vents was the storage-room from which John was busy working. He had arrived early on the second day of the job. He had already taken down most of the ceiling, which was good. It was just more time for him to *play* later on. He had taken down all the boards with the exception of the ones with wiring through them. Those would take some time to disconnect and remove. And with it being this early in the morning, he had all day to spend on tha tlittle project.

It had been an hour since he arrived that morning. He was busy removing a nail from one of those old boards with some wiring running behind it when he damn near lost his balance when a key from the organ was struck.

He walked over the one of the small openings of the wooden vents. Another key was struck, this one seemign louder thatn the first. His view was blocked by this end, so John moved to the other side of the room to get a better look at the organ. He looked down but there was no one there.

John sat back and... .

"John," a woman called out to him from below. "John. I'm down here honey."

Standing back in the same place, John looked down at the floor and what he saw stopped his breath. He couldn't believe his eyes. Standing between one of the aisles was his departed wife. Sharon, was her name. She had died two years ago from cancer. And now she stood within these walls and looked up at her husband.

John stood, frozen, as the two of them looked at each other. Even from the far up, John could see the dead grey color of Sharon's eyes.

He stood there for what semed forever. She was horrible. And yet beautiful all the same. She was the same girl with whom he had fallen in love with. He could see it. Even through the rot and decay. He could see it.

And there was a smell. The smell of rotting skin, and wet soil, and over all *death*. He could smell it even as high as he was.

"Come to me, John. I have something to give you," Sharon says and raises her hand. Within her closed dead fist was a single rose. John went down to her. Down the steps, through a hallway, and out to where his dead wife stood. You could say he was somewhat *hypnotized*.

"Sharon," John said as he looked at her. He stood at the end of the aisle. Looking in disbelief. And for reasons that could not be explained, he was holding a hammer. "This just can't be real."

"I have something to give you, my darling," Sharon says with the sweetest voice. She held out the rose to John and ask's him: "Be mine, John. Be my Valentine."

She moved towards him.

That hammer fell heavy to the floor.

5

As the afternoon came, the sky turned back to that dark red color again. The clouds were as white as ever, and the sun still shined brightly. Shinning its warm light through the blood red sky. And a breeze picked up. Not at all cold, but warm. As warm as that sun light.

And the city seemed silent. It was as if every person walking, or driving, were all locked within a day of silence. That was until a man driving a blue pick-up truck ran into a car waiting at a Stop sign. That was the first. There were other wrecks quickly after. For minutes on end all you could hear throughout the city of Fredericksburg was the sound of cars crashing. As well as the many sirens.

The city had gone into a state of chaos. And with all the destruction, there was no time to ask *why*? Everywhere that you could turn, there were wrecks, and screams. Horns blowing. Glass breaking. Pure chaos.

And then the dead came.

6

They came by the hundred. Breaking open their coffins. Digging their way out of that six feet of wet mud. Dirty, grey, rotted hands reached out of the ground and into the red light of that day. Few of them were infested with worms and maggots. Squirming and falling back to the ground as their *host* left them.

It didn't take long for the people driving by (and without wrecking their cars), to see these corpses walking, or running, down the street.

The first to get hit was a woman driving a Caravan with her two children riding in the backseat. She slammed on her breaks and came to a screeching stop. Thick, hot tar tracks ran to the rear tires. The woman sat in her Caravan on William St. and stared ahead of her with her mouth open. She was in total disbalief over what she was seeing. One of the dead stood within her Caravans way on the street. Staring right at her with his dead, grey eyes.

One of her two children saw the horrid looking man and started to scream. "MOMMY! MOMMY! WHAT IS THAT?" Then her other child started to cry and scream as well. "MOMMY! MOMMY! MOMMY!..." And that was all she could take. She turned and yelled at her two children. She told them to "SHUT IT!" and they did. She turned back to look at the man in the road and he was no longer standing in front of the car. Now he was standing beside her drivers side window and looking in.

He held out his hand. Dead and rotted and dirty. And within his hand was a rose. Where he had acquired it, this woman did not want to know.

"Be mine," the dead man said to her with a smile. He then smashed the window with one punch. The woman in the Caravan screamed (as well as her two children), and stomped on the accelerator. The dead man's arm tore right off and landed next to his feet. Green and yellow liquid came rushing out. As well as hundreds of maggots squirming from within the liquid. The dead man watched with such fierce hate as the Caravan sped away.

In a massive rush, all the flower shops in the downtown area of the *Burg'* were overrun with the living dead. They smashed the front windows, and display cases. They grabbed at every flower that they could get there dead, cold hands on. Some of the owners got away. And some became that special *Valentine*, and were dragged away. Broken arms and broken legs. Torn flesh and the smell of death filled the streets and air.

Just shortly after the woman in the Caravan sped away, another car came racing down William St. and ran into one of the living dead. He smashed against the windsheild, then rolled over the top of the car. Crashing down hard on his head and cracking open his skull. Half of his face tore off. The car that hit the dead man went crashing into a one way street sign. The driver went through what remained of the windsheild. The skin of his forehead tore open. And his left leg snapped in half.

All over the city, people were attacked by the living dead. Arms, legs, and necks were broke. Eyes gouged out. Tongues ripped apart. Cars busted into. And every victim, every *Valentine*, suffered the same fate. Dragged back to a muddy, dark grave. Dragged by their broken arms or legs. Taken to their new home with their new valentine with a rose placed in their hair.

The Falmouth bridge leading out of the city was jammed with cars. (As it tends to be sround rush hour). But only this time, the many drivers sitting in their cars had a lot more to worry about than to just make it across that bridge. Today, they would be lucky if they made it *alive* And to make matters worse, there just had to be a wreck at the intersection at the other end.

Bodies lay dead and bloodied on the pavement. There was a fire truck. An ambulance. And two Stafford county police cars. The two officers had to walk to the scene than drive.

An accident like this was bound to happen when you have a city overrun with dead people running every which way while trying to give away a rose (or whatever flower they could find), and make that one *unlucky* person their very own valentine. And they *will* make you theirs. That is if they can *catch* you first.

As all the drivers sat in their cars waiting for the wreck to clear, and as the fine men and women in uniform did *their* best to clean up the carnage, a mob of the living dead came rushing across the bridge.

More glass shattered. More bones broken. Some of the living dead ran towards the intersection. Both officers saw them coming and immediately opened fire. People screamed. Blood was shed. The afternoon went on.

7

His neck had been broken. Both wrists too. And now he was being dragged through a cemetery. He did not know which one it was. He did not even know where *he* was. But John could see her. Her dead and rotted hand held onto his ankle and dragged him along the cold ground. He knew that he was paralyzed. He knew it from the second that her dead hands had made his head turn ever so sharply. A fast pain that sent him to the church floor. It had happened after he took the rose from her. And right after she shed a lonely tear and told him to *kiss* her one last time.

She said that she was lonely. She said that she had missed him. And she had ran her cold fingers through his hair. And John had remembered all those late nights together with Sharon, so close to him, and waking in the morning light with her in his arms.

They stopped.

Sharon turned and looked down at him. Her eyes were so grey in color and full of hate. Worms and maggots squirmed out of her skin. She smiled.

"Were home now," she told John. He wanted to see but couldn't move his neck (let alone his arms). Another sign of being paralyzed. All john could do is look up at *her*, and up at that dark red sky.

The sky is red. The goddamn sky is red.

Those were Johns last thoughts while alive. Then, the two of them went in. One hard *thump* into her grave. John felt pain run through his legs as he hit that open casket. Sharon jumped on top of him and pulled the casket door. Closing the two of them in together. She laid on top of John and whispered in his ear.

"Be mine," she said.

And then the world went black.

8

Jim had gone inside his house after spilling his coffee. Unaware of the HELL that awaited him. He had no idea of the events that was to transpire that day. But it wouldn't matter anyway. Jim never lived to see the start od the next hour.

Upon entering his house, he knew that he was not alone. It wasn't just the *feeling* of knowing that someone else was in the house with him, there were signs. The kitchen door was closed. And the sound of someone walking on that hard kitchen floor could not be ignored. And then there was the smell. Something burning.

Jims first thought was to leave and contact the police by using his neighbors phone. Which really wouldn't have done any good since his neighbors were having some problems of their own.

"Jim."

A voice. So familiar.

"Jim! Come in here. I have got something for you, my darling."

It was *her*. It was Emma. She was here. With Jim. In *their* house. And the only thing that stood between the two of them was a few inches of wood that stood as the kitchen door. And now Jim stands before it. Sweating and shaking. He waited for something (anything), to happen.

She moved and stood directly on the other side of that kitchen door. Jim looked down and could see the shadow of Emma's feet. His heart began to beat hard. He thought he was scared (even though he didn't *feel* scared).

"Jim."

Her voice again. Calling from behind that wooden door. And it *is* her. Even though her voice sounds *different*. Not human. Alien. And... .

He needed to say something. And so he said the first thing that came to his shaking mind. "Emma? Are you alright?"

It was as if she had never died. As if the last few months were a dream and he just *now* awoke.

"You sound sick. Would you like me to get some medicine, honey?"

"JIM!" Emma screamed and slammed her fists against the kitchen door. Jim jumped back and placed a hand against his heart. He was scared now. There was no mistaking it.

"Come in here my darling husband. I have got something for you."

She backed away from the door. The shadow of her feet falling away behind the white painted door. Jim built up his courage and went in. Went in with force. Marching his way into the kitchen. Pushing the door open, slamming it against the wall, hard enough to leave a crack. Jim stood face to face with his dead wife, Emma.

Jim felt love and sorrow run through his heart. Looking at her made him remember all those lost years that they had spent together. All those holidays, summer vacations, and evenings alone together. It all came back to him. All at once.

"Emma, it... . I mean, is it really you?"

"Yes. And I have come back to you with a gift," Emma says and stands next to the kitchen table. She pulls out a chair. "But first, why don't you come and sit down and eat some breakfast."

Jim looked at the table. It was set with plates, spoons, forks, cups, and *roses*. The cups were filled with orange juice. And the plates were covered with dirt. Black dirt. The same that was all over Emma's clothes. The same dress and shoes of which she had been buried in.

And there was something on the stove. Something burning in a pot. Dark steam rose from top of it. Jim moved from around the table and towards the steaming pot. Emma watched him with eager dead eyes. Her skin was a pale white. And there was the smell of death. But not just from her. There was something else.

What Jim saw made his stomach turn , and he almost keeled over and let loose. Cooking in that pot was a rabbit. It once had been white, but now was covered with its own blood. Pouring out of open stomach. There were rabbit guts and worms boiling within ths rabbits blood. And the fur was burning as well.

"Are you hungry, my love?" Emma asked him.

"Emma," Jim turned and looked at her, "what have you done?"

Emma went to him and placed her arms around him.

"Are you ready for your gift?" she asks hium. "Your Valentines Day gift."

"No, Emma. Get out. Get out of here... . NOW!"

Jim tried to release her hands from him. But as soon as he moved, his head spun around. Snapping his neck. He fell back and hit the handle to the pot on the stove. It turned over, spilling the dead cooked rabbit and some hot oil over some hand towels. Within minutes, the entire kitchen was in flames.

No firemen came to the scene. And no ploice, or ambulance. The entire house burned and took nearly all of that morning to do just that. Some people who saw the burning house *did* try to call for help, but those calls were cut short due to the living dead coming after them with a rose and a death wish.

Blood filled the streets of Fredericksburg. Most of the blood was made in a long trail that ran from houses and cars. Leading to cemeteries somewhere. Pieces of torn skin and broken bone could be found within these long bloody trails. And the screams and moans of the unlucky Valentines Day victims were heard throughout the city.

9

Heather had awoken to the sound of the phone ringing. It had been ringing for quite some time. And she was slow to answer it.

Heather had slept half the day away. And as she sat up in her bed, she checked the time. It was well into the afternoon. 2:38 p.m. It came as a shock to her that she had slept so long. She answered the phone.

"Hello?" she asks rather sleepy.

"Heather, its mom!"

"Hey, where are you? I just got up and... ."

Do not leave the house!" her mother shouted in her ear. "DO YOU HEAR ME, YOUNG LADY?"

"Mom, whats this al about? What dod I do?"

But there was no answer from her. Just the sound of breaking glass and her mother screaming on the other end. A mans voice was heard. "Be mine," he said. And then the sound of someone choking. And then the line went dead.

Heather got out of bed and looked out her bedroom window. She could see nothing wrong (at first), but she could *hear* sirens coming from all directions. She looked a few seconds longer, then she saw smoke rising into a *red* sky. Black smoke. Black smoke that was rising from Jim's burned house. And then she saw her neighbor, Anne Towers running down their block from a man holding a rose and yelling for her to: "Be mine! Be mine!"

There was a noise from outside her bedroom door. Heather stood looking st it for a second or two. She was not alone.

"Who's there?" she calls out. "Dad? Did you take off from work today?"

"Let me in, Heather. Just let me in," a voice says. A familiar sound. One that she has not heard in quite some time. Only it was different. Deeper. Mean. Heather did not like the sound of it.

Jeffery. Jeffery is here. In the house and with me.

"Jeffery?" Heather asks with uncertainty.

"Yes, Heather. It is me. And I want to see you. I *need* to see you. Don't you want to see me?"

This couldn't be real. Could it? She didn't know. Heather thought that maybe she was still dreaming. That maybe she had never even woke up. But then she realized that even in her sleep, she hadne even dreamt of anything. And she was one of those types that *always* remembered her dreams.

She walked to the door and grabbed the handle. There was the sound of feet, backing away and down into the hallway. Heather, not really knowing what to do, laid back down on her bed. She wanted to sleep again. That was all she could think now. Just to sleep and wake up a new.

There was a long period of silence. Almost too long. And then Jeffery called to her again.

"Heather. Heather."

She heard his voice from the other side of that door. She heard his voice echo through the air vents of the floor and ceiling. "Heather, Heather, Heather... ." Jeffery called out to her. She covered her ears as his voice became louder. And louder. And... . LOUDER!

"Stop it!" Heather screams.

She got off her bed, opened her bedroom door, and ran right into Jeffery's dead arms. He had stood, waiting for her with the roses that he had left for her in the car. And as soon as she was within his grasp, Jeffery hugged her with such incredible strength that her spine cracked.

The smell of decay made her want to vomit. And she wanted to. But more than that, she wanted him to let her go. She felt something *move* onto her face. A worm. A yellow one that had fallen from Jeffery's decaying skin. Then more came out. Dozens. They crawled over her nose, cheeks, and lips. Heather kept her mouth tightly shut. Even though she wanted to cry out.

One of the worms crawled up and into her eye. And that was more than enough for her to handle.

"LET GO OF ME!" she screamed.

She tried to break free. She was panicking. She was *squirming*. And Jeffery *did* let her. For only a second, before he slammed his ex-girlfriend against the wall. The back of her head made a small hole, and some of the pictures on the wall shook and moved out of place.

"What did I do? Why are you hurting me?" Tears were running now. And she was trying to hold it together. She was scared. So very scared. Heather looked at him. Her dead ex.

This is impossible. Your dead. I was there when they buried you.

There was a deep pain coming from the back of her head. As well as something *wet* running down the back of her neck.

Just don't think about that. *It's the least of your problems now.* If Heather had seen a drop of blood, she would have fainted right then and there. But she didn't have to worry about fainting. For Jeffery would soon fix all her fears.

"I have something for you, Heather." Jeffery held up his hand with the roses in them. They were now crushed to almost nothing.

"Be mine," she hears his dead voice say to her. "Be mine."

All was quiet in the house for a moment. Then Heather screamed.

The Way Things Were

1

I live in a small town. Quiet. Suburban. Church on every corner. (That's a bit of an exaggeration, but I think that you can read between the lines). Houses with white picket fences. You know the type of twon that I am talking about. Everyone knows each other. And the police station (which seems to *always* sit right in center of everything), find that the biggest crime is some local hothead vandalizing one of the brick walls of the high school. Or grocery store.

These men and women make their rounds in their blue and white cars, letting the citizens know that they are here if needed. Just call that number in the yellow pages and they will be there before the crime is finished. (Or before the person who has commited the crime has time to get away). Because it is like I said before, this is a small town. Where everyone knows each other.

Pretty lame, isn't it? Go on. You can laugh if you want. I don't mind. I used to laugh at it myself. But those days are long gone. Especially after that one afternoon while lying in bed with my wife. After we had heard from my brother Bill, about our good friends, Scott and Nancy. Two friends who we all thought we knew. But were wrong. *Dead* wrong.

2

There were eight of us. Myself and Kim (now my wife). My brother Bill, and his girl, Stacey. Beth and Leland. And Scott and Nancy. We had all gone to school together. As far back as elementary. We had all gone through the good times, as well as the bad, together. Parties. Drugs. Sex. And we would all joke that we were the real life version of the show Beverly Hills 90210. But then again, I am sure that a whole lot of people out there did the same within their own group.

It was going to be us. Us eight against the world. Living in the same small town that we grew up in. And living that all American dream. Good job. A nice house. A cookout at the end of every week. (Preferably on a Sunday afternoon, and after church service. Of course). Marriage, with a few kids. Retirement plan. A weeks vacation to the beach. It was all going to be so perfect. And it would have if it wasn't for... .

Let me go back to the events that lead up to what happened. I am married now (happily, if you were wondering), and had recently moved into the house that

I and my wife live in now. Although at the time that I am speaking of, we were still engaged. In fact, our three year anniversary is coming up. So cheers to the two of us, and to any other happily married couple about to celebrate their own anniversary too. But let me get back to what I was saying before.

It was one month to the day. And I just happened to find myself sitting at a bar with Scott, sharing a pitcher.

"So, how are you and the missus?" I ask him. We were both pretty buzzed by then.

"Were doing great," Scott says with a smile. "The wedding invitations go out this Saturday. I can hardly wait." He says, but with a hint of distaste, doubt, or maybe it was *fear*.

"Why Saturday?" I ask. I mean, that just sounded strange for me to hear. It was a Tuesday evening. So why not just send the invitations out the next day?

"Because that way the two of us can do it together. And *she* will then know that I won't make a single mistake. She will know that everything is going according to plan." Scott takes a sip of his beer. Then adds: "Her plan."

"And I am going to guess that Nancy's plan is to tie you down and make you her... ."

"All right wise-ass," Scott says with a smile. "Just drink your beer would ya."

And I did. And he drank his. And then we both drank more. And soon enough, the rest of the gang had joined us. Everyone had gotten off from work. And now it was there turn to kick back a few at our favorite pub.

By the way, I know I didn't mention it before, but I am manager at one of the three local banks here in town. My wife is a secretary at a very successful law firm.

(We have quite a few of them in town. For some unholy reason).

My brother Bill and Scott are in the auto repair business. And Nancy, Beth, and Stacey all work at the Motel out by the interstate. Right on the edge of our small town.

Everyone works days. Although Nancy sometimes leaves work an hour (sometimes two hours), late. But other than that, it is a set working schedule. Now, if we could all get the same days off, then hell, we would be the envy of all the other hard working suckers out there who are trapped working thse long weekend hours. Wouldn't we?

Don't answer that. Because I have much more to tell you. And believe me when I tell you that I am *very* grateful for you to be listening.

We all sat at that bar for most of the night. Which was uncommon for us to do. We were all good (usually) at keeping a safe limit.But this one night, well I guess that sometimes you just have to say 'the hell with it,' and cut loose.

Scott and Nancy were (without a doubt), the life of the party that night. Laughing and loving each other. Holding hands. Enjoying life. They were *the* couple. *Perfect*, as some people would say.

And that was the way things were. For all of us. And for that last month we all had together. Everyone laughing and loving one another. Work, church, cookouts. We were living the dream. *Still* are. Only now... .

3

The last time that I talked to Scott was on a Friday afternoon. I had been giving him rides to and from work. He and Nancy had to resort to the use of one car by then, and Nancy insisted that she be the one to use it being that the two of them worked in opposite directions. And also after being told by Nancy that she was pregnant.

Scott had said that the other car was in the shop. But neither my brother, Bill (or myself), had ever seen the car in the shop. And Bill was a little pissed about knowing that Scott would go to some other shop. "Don't you think that Scott would haved told me about any problems that was happening? Don't you think so?"

And my answer was yes. But it did seem odd that Scott would lie about something that would easily be *seen* as a lie. And I would guess that after pursuing the matter more, that that was the reason that Scott had told me another lie. That the car was in another shop up town.

"Because they have these parts that I need, and that I am not good at working with. So I took it up there to have this specialist work on it. Alright?" Scott had asked me a little irritably. And so I just said that it was fine and that I was just looking out for the two of them. And that was all.

"I know," Scott says to me before he breaks down and cries.

To see Scott cry shocked me. I have known this guy for most of my life and had never seen him drop a single tear. (Well, unless he had been laughing his ass off at one of us in the group. Which just so happened to be quite a lot). So I pull my car into a parking lot and turn off the engine. But I *did* leave the radio on. But low. I guess that the light soft sound of classic rock was going to make this situation a little bit more easy for the two of us to sit through. And I was right. (For once). But before I could say a single word to Scott, I just sat and waited for him to calm himself down a bit. It didn't take long. But it sure as hell felt like a long time.

"Are you ready to tell me what is going on?" I asked.

"Yes. I guess so," Scott says back to me while he uses a shaking hand to wipe his cheeks dry. Then he tells me. But with his head down and his hands (still shaking), sitting in his lap. His first few words were low. And I had to ask him to repeat what he had just told me. Because I thought I *had* heard him correctly. But I did *not* want to believe it.

"I said that Nancy is seeing someone else. Did you hear me that time?" Scott asked with a bit of anger in the tone of his voice. So I said that I *did* hear him, and that what he had just told me could not be true. Could it?

"Yes, its true. Everything I am about to tell you is true. I jut don't know where to start. It is all happening so fast and I really don't know what I should do about any of it. What am I going to do?" Scott asked me and almost starts crying again. But then he gets control with one deep breathe. And as soon as I saw that he was himself again, *really* himself again, I say to him:

"Why don't you just start from the beginning."

"Alright," he says and looks out the passenger window. "It all started three weeks ago. You remember that one night when we were all at the bar and getting hammered? You rememeber that right?"

I acknowledged that I did and Scott continues.

"That night Nancy and I made love when we got home. And I cannot imagine how I had missed it before. But after we were done, and we were lying next to each other, I noticed what I had thought to be a bruise on the loweer left side of her neck. And so I asked her about it. And she said that yes, it was a bruise. A bruise that she had got when she had to bend down to get her pen that she had dropped under her desk. And that when she had come back up, she had hit the corner of a desk. She had said that it had happened just that day. 'You didn't see it earlier at the bar?' she asks me. And so I say no. In fact, none of us did since her hair was covering it up. And so I just left it alone. You know? I didn't want to argue with her. Especially after we... . Well, you know what I am saying right?"

And again I said that yes, I understood. And Scott continues.

"So a few days go by. Three at the most. And that damn bruise is pretty much gone by then. But let me tell you something my friend, a real bruise doesn't just go away in three days. Maybe three weeks. But not three days."

And it was at that moment that I knew where Scott was going with this story. And I had the strongest compulsion to tell him to stop. That I really didn't want to know anymore. But then, what kind of friend would that have made me? A pretty lousy one, I suppose.

"I am sure that you already know what I am going to tell you about that so called bruise on Nancy's neck. Don't you?" Scott asked while staring right into my green eyes. I only sat and waited for hium to tell me. "It was a goddamn lovers bite. Can you believe that?"Scott ased me and lowers his head again.

There was a moment of silence. I could tell that he was trying his best to hold his composure. Which I was grateful for. I can only imagine just how hard it must have been for him to tell me these things. But in a way, I kind of already knew. I had been in a deep relationship with a girl right before my wife. And I will never forget the pain that I had felt when I had found out what she had been doing when I wasn't around.

The only thing that I could tell Scott was at least I was the only one who knew. Because when I had found out that my old girl was getting off with some other guy, I was the *last* to know. Everyone knew. Even people in the next town knew. And so I had pitched that little bit of knowledge to Scott. Not that it really helped all that much. In fact (and now that I think about it), it had made things worse.

"I don't know the guys name. But I have *seen* him plenty of times. Nancy does him after her shift is up from work. That is why she has been coming home an hour late everyday." Scott was beginning to cry again. And his hands began to shake. Again. "And she's *not* pregnant. She is using that story just so she can use the car. Since she wrecked the other one."

Scott was looking at me again. His eyes were red from the tears and his cheeks were wet again.

"Do you want to know what happened to my truck? Should I tell you?"

I replied no. But he told me the story anyway. He tells me how Nancy had left the bar next to her work one night, seeing *triple*. She had ran the truck into a ditch down the road from their home.

Scott tells me that the engine is beyond repair. And asks me if I know just how lucky Nancy was to have walked away without a DUI.

"Stupid bitch!" Scott snarls and slams his fist on his leg. "I wish now that she *had* gotten a goddamn DUI. I wish that something... ANYTHING... Would happen to her. Something to wreck her day. No, NO! Her life."

And as I sat there and listened, I had a feeling. One of those feelings that you get deep down in your gut. It tells you that something just isn't right. I mean, the whole situation that I had found myself in wasn't right. But it was the *tone* of Scott's voice that got me. More so than the look of hate that filled hie eyes. I had never seen him lok that way. Or sound that way either.

"So, I am going to assume that you have talked to her about all of this?" I ask.

"NO!" Scott says sharply. "Haven't you been listening to me. She doesn't know that I know. And I am terrified of what will happen if I do confront her about it. I'm afraid." Scott took a moment and regathered himself. "I'm afraid that if I do say something, that she will leave me. And I can't be alone. Not now. Not at this stage in our relationship. We've been together for so long, that I can't imagine a life without her. In fact, I *won't*."

I started my car. It was getting late and all I wanted to do now was to get Scott home as well as myself. Which I know sounds insensitive. But to hell with it. There was no getting through to the guy. And what I really mean by that was no matter what I had to say to the guy, he wasn't going to listen. So I kept my mouth shut and drove him home.

4

It was Bill who had discovered the bodies. It wasn't hard for him to see. The curtains were open just enough for him to look down at Scott lying across Nancy on their living room floor. He had told me that he just stood there and stared at the two dead bodies until he felt sick.

The morning paper had called it a murder suicide. And that good ole Scott had murdered his wife before taking his own. There was even a report that evening on the news. They had said that two high school sweethearts were found dead in their home in College Heights. That it was a MASSACRE. That it was TRAGIC. That Nancy had been killed in a lovers quarrel.

But we knew different. The six of us. We knew different. Especially me. Because what had really happened that night was this: Scott had confronted Nancy abour her new *fling*, and thigs got heated. So heated that the two of them had literally lost their heads and pulled a knife on each other.

Nancy had three stab wounds. One to her stomach. And the other two just above her left breast. Scott had one. And it wasn't to any part of his chest either. It was right through the neck. Right through his jugular. And it was upon finding the two cold bodies that Bill saw that knife, still held by Nancy's right hand, and sticking into Scott's neck as he lay dead on top of her.

And the blood.

"All that blood. It surrounded them. That alone was enough to make me sick," Bill had told me in a dazed state of mind. He was never the type to stand strong at the sight of blood. He would always go weak in the knees. Always had. Even as a child playing games and wrestling around. The first drop of that red liquid made his stomach turn.

But that was then. And this is now. For better or worse, this is now. And time *does* move on. At least most of the time.

5

It was two weeks after the murders had happened. Kim and I live right down the street from where Scott and Nancy's house is. (Well, what used to be there house). And so it was never really a bother for me to drive Scott to and from work everyday.

Their house sits on Stafford Avenue. And I had used that road as a main route home. Been using it for quite some time. But after Scott and Nancy's *incident*, I had avoided that street all together. Kim didn't seem to mind. She had been (and still is), very upset over the new of how her two friends had tragically ended their lives together.

But as I was saying, it had been two weeks of avoiding that street all together. And I felt that two weeks was time enough for me to get face what had happened. And so it was on a Saturday afternoon that I decided to take a walk. Not a very long one. But a nice stroll down the street. And I will never forget how nice the weather was that day. Not a cloud in the sky. And a cool seventy five degrees. Perfect. I couldn't have asked for anything better.

Their house is five blocks from mine. And by the third block on my walk, I could already see the FOR SALE sign sitting on the edge of the front lawn. And within no time at all, I was standing right next to that sign with that eight hundred number on it, and the cheesy picture with the real-estate agent grinning away like an insane person. I have always hated those pictures. Probably always will.

But there I stood, looking at Scott and Nancy's house. Now vacant and waiting to be alive again. Sitting quietly, and *dark*.

I stood there and just looked. I observed everything. But nothing in particular. And then I noticed something (but for a minute I believed it to be my imagination), so I walked a little ways closer to get a better look. I had seen something from the living room. It was still hard to see. Even with as much sun that was shinning, those empty rooms of the house were darker. And so that made it harder to see inside from where I was standing on the front lawn. And I dared to not go any farther. I wasn't sure why. I just had this feeling coming from deep in my stomach. It was like the day that my brother had come by and found the bodies, and how the longer he looked through that window, the sicker he felt. And now the same was starting to happen to me. Only this time I *was* going to be sick.

My stomach began to hurt. And my hand started to shake. And I broke into a sweat. But I still looked on.

Through the darkness behind that window. And I started nto have thoughts. Scot and Nancy, covered in their blood. Dead on their living room floor. And the silence that had followed after the fighting was done.

I felt sick. And I wanted to *be* sick, but then I saw her. As I tell you now, I saw Nancy. She was standing in the center of that darkened room and staring back at me. Her eyes were cold and hateful. My hands began to shake even harder. And I could hear a voice. *Her* voice. Like a whisper in my ear. And she said to me: "Join us. Join us."

I hunched over, and as I did I felt a chill run over my body. My head began to spin, and as it did, I heard the front door creep open. Just enough so that when I had looked over I could see Scott looking at me from behind that little amount of opened space. His eyes held the same hate as Nancy's. And I could hear *his* voice now. He spoke in unison with hers. "Join us," the two of them said. "Join us."

I finally fell to my knees and was sick. I saw my lunch spread on Scott and Nancy's lawn. And afterwards, when I felt strong enough, I ran. Off that lawn and down Stafford Avenue. Away from that house. And away from Scott and Nancy. I have not been bak since.

6

Memories. Memories are are all we have to remind us of times past. And the memories of my two friends that I *want* to remember are *not* of the end of their lives (or afterlife), but of their life together, and with us. Not very often, but every once in a while I will think of my two friends and about the way things were. And how happy I was to have had that time together.

The Songs Of The Cemetery Trees

1

Those songs could be heard within the cold wind that ran through the cemetery at midnight. The sound of a thousand voices singing their songs of heartbreak and joy. Of love and hate. Of life. And of death.

Through the rain, sun, heat, and cold. And from summer to winter, these old oak trees sing the songs of those who are laid to rest here in this old cemetery called Tree Top Hill. Called so because when looked upon from a distance, it is not a cemetery that is seen, but a wall of those old oak trees.

Every small town in America has their own ghost story. And this is ours.

2

It is said that when one hears the songs of the cemetery trees, that death is right around the corner. Waiting to take you away. Never has these songs gave away as to *how* these people will die. Or when. And *that* must be the most terrifying of all for whoever hears those dreadful songs.

This is a small town (as I said before), and this particular *legend* has been around since way before my time (and your as well, as I am sure), and so when one of the twonfolk passes away (more like murdered), there is always that inevitable question.

Does anybody know what songs were heard before said passing came about?

And to answer the question, no one knows. Since the one who passes has never speaks a word to anyone of *what* music is ringing through their ears in the days leading to their impending death. But even with that little bit of knowledge to the story, people will believe whatever superstition they have grown up knowing.

Yes, I said it. Superstition. Folklore. Urban legends. Whatever it may be that you want to call it. The *ghost* story was all the same to me. Just stories to tell your friends while sitting around while stoned out of your mind. Drunk off your ass. Or sitting alone with your loved one and snuggling warmly together on the couch. Or in the bed.

"Rediculous," my mother would tell me. "Just stories people tell each other as a joke for a smoke." Whatever that expression means is beyond me. But I believed her. And I believed it all to be trash talk. That was until three days ago when I heard those old oak trees singing their death songs for me.

3

It was a warm Sunday morning when I heard the music. At first I thought that maybe my neighbors were playing some *classical* recordings really loud. It reminded me of something that resembled opera. But I had quickly learned that that was not the case. Neither one of my neighbors were home.

I then thought that there was some kind of gathering at the university (I happen to live just one block away), but then remembered that it was spring break. So I took my morning shower before leaving for work. And by the time that I was dressed and walking out my apartment door, the music had stopped.

That Monday afternoon (I think it was around three) I heard a womans voice. And as clear as a bird chirping on a clear sunny day. I just so happened to be in my car and had just passed the Tree Top Hill Cemetery. I damn near collided into the car sitting at the red light in front of me. I would guess that it was a two, if not three, inches from the cars rear bumper, when I came to that abrupt stop. I was shaking. And theback of my neck had broke out into a cool sweat. But I must tell you, I wasn't sweating from almost causing an accident. I was sweating from the sound o that woman's voice. So real it sounded. And for a moment I thought that there was a woman in the car with me. It was that feeling that you get when you can *sense* someone else's presence.

But of course, I was alone. And I had dismissed the thought as soon as the light turned green, and the car (that had no idead how lucky they were), began to move.

Tuesday night I took a walk. I cannot say for sure what time it was. But I know that it wasn't late.

On my walk I found myself standing before the entrance to the Tree Top Hill Cemetery. It was no accident. I knew where I was going.

The steel gates were closed and locked (which I know was for the best), but I still had a very clear view of those old oak trees and the hundreds of grave markers that filled the ground. There were no voices heard. But I *did* hear the sound of a piano playing softly from deep within that darkened cemetery that night. And I have to say that if I wasn't so sure that those notes being played by those old oak trees were for my impending death, then I would have actually enjoyed hearing it.

I walked back home shortly after. Only, a little faaster this time.

And now I sit hear at my desk, in my apartment, writing this little short story. Why? The answer is this. Because if the story about the cemetery trees *is* true, then I want *you* to know about it. Whoever you are, I want you to know what *has* happened, and *is* happening. And maybe (just maybe) you will learn from it.

It has started to rain outside. And I am beginning to hear the faint sound of violins and a trumpet playing alongside a piano. I just heard a deep roar of thunder.

And a strong gust of wind has picked up. And my name...
I can hear my name being called again.

That woman's voice is calling me again. I think she is
telling me to come. Or maybe *she* is coming. I can't tell.
The sound of the rain...

There is a pain under my left arm. And I feel as
though I am going to choke. The music is becoming
louder. I feel a cold sweat on my face and neck. And now
I am only writing with my right hand. My left arm is
numb and...

This is it. This is the end.

And if this may be the last line that I write...

May God have mercy on my soul.

One Rose

1

He stood on the edge of the hill and looked down. From up here, he could see the entire town. It was small, and it became even smaller high up on this hill. Smoke was rising from the many buildings that had been hit during the long battle. *They* had survived the fight. But the loss was almost too great for their freedom.

Most of the fires had been put out. But the ones that still burned seemed unable to contain. And even up here, away from the ruined town, he could still hear the sound of those who cry and scream over their loss.

When will the wasr be over?

It had been two years going, and there seemed to be no end.

The casualties were becoming too great to think of. Because everyone who lived was effected by this war of greed. And wasn't that what it is all about? Yes. And isn't that what *all* wars are ultimately about? Maybe. But he decided that he would go on and give both questions and great big YES.

But as he stood on the edge of this hill, his thoughts could not remain on the *why's* and *how's* of war. Because there was a smell. The smell of death. Blood and skin. Some of it torn, and some of it burned, off of the bones and every muscle of all the soldiers who had lived and fought for the good of their nation. And these dead men were not just lying on the streets of his small hometown. They were right below him. Lying on this hill that ran high overlooking the streets of this town whose own freedom had been under question.

This hill started its downward slop at the end of a plantation. Once owned by the states governor, was now the setting for the allies to set camp. But that plan would only stay strong for the first day of battle. The women and children were told to stay among the grounds of the plantation till the battle was ended. The thought was that this huge hill, covered by thousands and thousands of roses, grown within the body of a deep rose bush, would keep the enemy at bay. And that would keep the women and children safe from any, and all, of harms way.

At onwe time this hill was celebrated by the entire town. It has always been the main attraction for this small town. It was a *wall* that seemed to run up, and up, high into the heavens above. The morning sun shines its bright light upon the multicolor of roses that sit as though in an *Impressionist* painting.

But now, after the long days of a bloody battle, this hill is no longer filled with that radiant beauty. Now, there is only the look rubble. And death.

On the second day of battle, there was an explosion. The men in the small town had stood in line on the top of this hill. They stood in arms, and had awaited for the rebels to try and take what would never be theirs. And all was working fine until cannons were fired and the ground beneath these brave men fell from beneath them. Nearly a hundred men had fallen into that massive rose bush. The pain that these men fell into can never be described.

As they fell, thorns tore into their skin. They dug deep into their veins and stomach. They tore into their necks. Cutting open their skin. Blood sprayed out of their bodies in all areas imaginable. Some of the men could *hear* the skin being torn from off of their bodies. Some of the men thought the sound to be that of tearing a piece of paper in half. And that sound of tearing flesh had blocked out everything else that was happening at that moment. Not even the cries of the men who had fallen were loud enough to block out the sound of ripping flesh.

And that is where those unfortunate men lay. Even now. On the day after the end of the battle. Those men, some struggling to get free from the entanglement of the rose bushes. And some simply awaiting for their death. *Praying* for it. And some of the men had finished the job themselves.

And it is on this early morning that he stands on the top of this hill and looks down upon the blood, fire, and the dying men below him. Pieces of torn flesh scattered all around. And what made this worse for him was the realization that the life he once knew was now over. He could not only see it, he could *smell* it. Because it was everywhere. And it has become too much for him to handle. He had never seen anything like what he has in the past few days. And he never wants to see it again. And now he has decided to end it.

"This life. This world. I cannot go through this pain no longer. It is ugly. And all that beauty, gone. And for what? FOR WHAT I ASK YOU?"

He pulls his own gun from the holster and cocks the trigger. And as he does, a burst of that morning sunlight comes through from behind some clouds passing by.

"I... ." And that was all he says before he sees it standing there. One rose standing alone within all the death and destruction. The sunlight shone down upon its full blossomed body. It was beautiful. And within that moment, he was reminded of the beauty that had once stood. And that all that death and destruction *will* fade away in time. And that life will rebuild all that was lost.

He lowered his gun. All intentions from moments before were now gone. Now, the only feeling he held was hope. Yes, there was beauty. And the pain will fade away. And he would not die until the life that he once knew was back. And that hill, which now holds only one rose, gave birth to the thousands that held it before.

The Bells Of St. Katherine

1

She came back again late one night in April. It had rained all day, and most of the evening. There was a cool chill in the air. And a thick blanket of fog had settled throughout the town. A town hidden deep within the mountains of Colorado.

The streets were visible for a block or two, then they disappeared into the cloudy whiteness. It was now two minutes to midnight and all was silent. All the doors were locked, and people could be seen peering out from behind their curtains. Eyes open wide. And scared to the bone. For the residents in this town live in fear. And the ones who dare to look upon into this cloudy night, wait for the bells of St. Katherine Church to toll midnight. And then *she* will come.

Everynight at the hour of eight, the bells will ring, letting the residents know that it was time to go home and to *stay* there. But there are always those few who don't listen. There were always those non-believers who didn't take heed to the rules of this town. And there were always bodies to be found the next morning. Sometimes deep in the woods. But most the time, the bodies (or body *parts*), are found on the streets and in front yards.

She is a secret that this town tries to keep. And secrets are well kept in a town such as this.

And on this night, and as the bells rang as the tall hand hit midnight, whoever was safely asleep in their bed was no longer asleep now. Three bells ringing together in unison. The sound that they made were long and deep.

Some people (upon being awakened by the sound of those bells), checked their windows and doors. And some people kneeled down beside their bed and prayed. And it is no srprise to find a cross in every house, and hanging on every bedroom wall.

It was on the twelfth ring that she appeared. A dark figure coming out of the thick fog, walking slowly down Main St. and hungry. She wears a long black dress and hides her face behind her long hair. Hair as black as the dress she wears.

She is so hungry and is on her hunt for the first kill. No one knows what she is. And it may be that she herself *doesn't* even know. But she *is* and has *always* been for as long as anyone who lives in this town knows. She was around back when the old-timers were children. And maybe longer than that. But the story differs. And now she walks the night. Slow and hungry.

Old Man Peters (a retired postal worker after forty years of service), saw her first that night. He had seen her before. Back in his childhood. And she looked as dead as she does now, this *cloudy* night.

As said before, her hair is long and black. Her skin is pale. But hidden beneath a brown coat of fur. Wet and muddy. Her eyes glowed a dark yellow. And her hands hung by her sides. Fingers stretched with long fingernails. Sharp, and covered with dirt and blood. And dried pieces of *meat*.

It sent chills over Old Man Peters to see her again. And his heart just about stopped when she stopped walking, turned in his direction, and looked right into his old eyes. Peters felt a sweat break out on his forehead, and he pulled the curtains to hide from the *monster* outside. But still, he looked from behind those curtains. And as he did this, she smiled at him. Her eyes glowing that sickly ellow as her lips widened. Peters could see her teeth peering out and over them. And it scared him more to see them. Fangs. Two on the top and two on the bottom. He couldn't tell if the other teeth were the same. And it didn't really matter. He just wanted it to end. And it did. But not in the way that he would have wanted it.

There just happened to be three grey rabbits that ran across Old Man Peters front yard as he was staring into those horrid yellow eyes of the Ghost Lady. (That was the name the townspeople called her) And as soon as she saw them, she was no longer concerned about Old Man Peters. She was dead set on those rabbits as they ran and stopped, at the sudden realization that they were being watched by another animal? As all animals do when they since danger in their path.

The Ghost Lady's smile faded into a sneer and she started to growl. And as she did, there was an uneasy tension as she planned her attack. The rabbits sat on that cool grass and waited. The Ghost Lady eyed each one of them... then attacked.

One hand reached down and grabbed the first rabbit by the neck. It snapped immediately as it was taken off the ground and into her mouth. Fangs bore deep into the rabbits stomach. Blood squirted into her mouth and down her chin. The crunching sound of bones being broken and flesh torn was all that was heard. The other two rabbits tried to run but The Ghost Lady was too quick and had them both in her grasp in seconds of seeing them flee. It was as though she took two steps and had them. It all happened so fast.

Old Man Peters looked in horror as blood ran out and down her chin. It ran over her bust hidden under the black dress that she wore. He stared out from behind the curtains as the Ghost Lady walked slowly away and into town. Her face and fingers covered with rabbit blood.

Pieces of rabbit flesh was thrown in al directions on his front lawn. A nice green lawn, now tie-dyed with dark red. (Christmas anyone?) Old Man Peters wouldn't allow himself to be bothered with how he would tend to the mess the next morning. Instead, he went to bed.

And as he lay there under his warm blankets, he could hear the howl of the Ghost Lady in the far away distance. That horrible sound made when her stomach was full. The morning sun never came soon enough for this small town hidden deep in the mountains of Colorado.

2

Bryant is a young twenty year old who is traveling his way across the country. He had started his journey from the great state of Washington, in the city of Olympia. He had traveled to (and through) California in a months time. It didn't do much for him. And it had made him miss being back home in Olympia.

He had saved and saved for this long journey since starting work at the small diner he had been employed at since the age of sixteen. Washing dishes at first, then, moved up to prep cook and ended as one of the diners main cooks. And it had taken him eight years since his first day working to save ten thousane fifty eight dollars and eight cents. He wasn't sure as to whee he was going. But he knew there was a new life for him somewhere. And Bryant couldn't wait to find it.

He rang the doorbell to the house that he would be renting a room out of. It is a nice house, just on the outskirts of town. Two story and white picket fence. Occupied by a family of six. Four kids watched over by two very loving parents.

Stan and Sherri Newman answered the door and let Bryant in. They were nice people indeed. But they also watched and checked Bryant all the same. Seeing if he would say, do, or look a certain way that would make them kick him out. But of course, he never did. And they showed Bryant to his room, downstairs and next to the laundry room.

Bryant had fallen asleep within minutes after unpacking. It had been a long ride. Trains and buses.

He was beat and hungry. But eating was going to have to wait. Besides, he would have plenty to eat when he started his new job in yet another diner. Well, that was just as soon as he went out and *got* another job. It had been over a month, and he was getting anxious.

He didn't get that job in another diner. Instead, Bryant got to work making pizzas at a famous Italian chain. The job paid nine dollars an hour. And it was there that Bryant would meet two other co-workers that he would have a great friendship with. Richard and Fiona. Richard would become a *brother* to him. And Fiona would become his girlfriend (as well as his wife).

Richard is the oldest of the three. Just turned twenty one two months before, and is the hook-up for drinks. He didn't mind though. It made Richard feel needed. And it got him more attention from some ladies.

They had told Bryant about the Ghost Lady one night after work. He had by now worked at the restaurant for two weeks, and the fact that he had not heard of the Ghost Lady by now was a miracle in itself.

Bryant thought Fiona and Richard to be mad. At first he thought it was a trick to scare him. And that would have been acceptable, but the two of them *really* believed. But even then, Bryant had kept a lot of his opinions to himself. He didn't want to offend them since they had taken a long time to tell him the story.

"Trust us, Bryant. The Ghost Lady is real. We just don't know what exactly she is," Fiona told him as she held his hand. The three were drunk. And Bryant could see the room start to spin. Richard sat quietly on the couch. He felt uncomfortable and scared. He could be somewhat of a pussycat at times. And so to shake off his nerves (as well as get his mind off of the Ghost Lady), he turned on the television.

"So when was the first time that you saw the Ghost Lady?" Bryant asked Fiona.

"I have never seen her myself. But my mom has. And I know some of the older folks in town who have. There is this old guy, his name is Jake Peters. But everyone calls him Old Man Peters. Anyway, the other day he was seen in a bar talking about how he not only saw the Ghost Lady, but said that there was a moment where they looked at each other. He swore that her eyes were so bright that he couldn't see anything for a few seconds after he looked away."

"Old Man Peters is full of it," Richard said. "He's just some old man who is lonely and has nothing better to do than bother everyone else with his bull crap stories," he says and continues to watch the game he found while channel surfing.

Fiona ignores this piece of mind from Richard and pays her attention back to Bryant. She was falling in love with him. As he was with her. They just couldn't say it to each other yet.

There was more to the story that Fiona told Bryant. And sh had waited to tell it after Richard had passed out on the couch.

"She was walking home with my dad one night when they were dating. They were halfway down her block when my mom saw her. She was standing on the corner of Maine St and third. My mom said that the Ghost Lady was wearing a black dress and was playing a violin. My mom said the she was playing the most lovely song, but had these dark yellow eyes. And my mother had told me that when the Ghost Lady saw her and my dad walking towards her, she smiled. And when she did, my mom saw these long fangs."

"Then what happened?" Bryant had asked. The two were lying close to each other on Richards bed. And as Fiona had talked, Bryant could only think of how good it was going to be to *touch* her, again.

"I don't know," Fiona answers. "That's all that my mom will tell me. And my dad won't say a word about the story. Weird huh?"

After the story they had *touched* each other for a long time. It was much needed. And afterwards the two fell fast asleep. They had both been working a lot lately. And they needed that bit of release.

The night was *still*. And the Ghost Lady walked the streets. Slowly and within the shadows of the night. And as soon as her belly was full, and the blood ran long down her chin and body, she howled to the bright moon overhead.

When Bryant awoke to the sound of the bells of St. Katherine Church ringing the hour of eight, he believed that he had dreamed it all. He had dreamt of awakening late in the night with Fiona still by his side. It was the sound of a howling coming from out in the woods that had disturbed his sleep. It echoed through the night sky. Bryant got out of bed and looked out the window. There was a thick fog that had settled outside. And within the fog he could see a dark figure. A woman. She wore a long black dress and had the palest skin he had ever seen. Her face was too hard to distinguish. But the shape looked to be that of a wolf. And he could *see* her eyes. They shone a dark sick yellow. And he waited for her to smile.

He wanted to see those fangs. But they never came. The Ghost Lady never smiled.

And it was all a dream? And that was what he told Fiona and Richard when the two of them had woken after him. Two hours after him.

According to one legend, the Ghost Lady was a mother of four who lived in the late 1800's. She was the wife of an abusive lumberjack, with whom had supposedly killed her while the two of them had journeyed deep into the woods to collect fire wood.

Her name was Evelyn Gray. A strict and loving mother. As well as a devoted wife. No matter how bad her husband treated her, she was always there for him. And for that, she had been murdered. Strangled, and left tied to a large tree.

She was buried in the cemetery behind St. Katherine church. Her husband did not attend the funeral. But weeks later he did, one very late night, go into the cemetery with a shovel and dig her grave open. But as the story goes, upon opening the coffin of his dead wife, he was dumbfounded to find that she was *not* there.

And it was shortly after, that the twonfolk could hear the sound of a wolf howling from deep in the surrounding forrest. From that night on, the town was haunted.

3

Bryant wanted to see the lady of the Ghost Lady now that he knew the story, and after having that dream. Richard and Fiona agreed and had made plans to take Bryant out that Friday night. It would have to be late. Well after town curfew. Which started everyday night at the stroke of eight by those bells. Those bells that echo their sound through the town and high into the mountains.

And if the townsfolk only knew that it was those very bells that awoke the Ghost Lady... .

That Friday saw a whole lot of rain. And by the time that Bryant, Fiona, and Richard went out there was a slight drizzle. Another thick fog had settled throughout the town, making their vision of the streets ahead of them rather difficult to see.

Between tall thick trees, and uncut grass, the cemetery sat in wait. At the entrance, the three of them stood and looked in. They would have to go about this very carefully. They knew that they wouldn't be seen, since they wore all black. Plus the thick fog added that extra touch. And after waiting for one of the two *men* in the group to make the first step, Fiona finally decided to grow her own set and stepped in.

"Well, come on you two. We don't have all night."

Bryant and Richard gave each other a quick look, shrugged their shoulders, and followed Fiona to the grave sight.

The Ghost Lady (Evelyn Gray) was laid to rest in the far back of the cemetery. To the left, and sitting under an oak tree. The grave marker was so old and weather worn that the inscription was no longer legible.

And there the three of them stood in silence and looked. Bryant was scaring himself. He kept thinking that the three of them were being watched. And even though all was silent, he thought he could hear the sound of someone (or something) moving around in that thick white fog. And he could see that Richard was doing the same.

Bryant thought it best to not say anything though.

So now they had found it. And now Bryant had *seen* it. So now what?

"Do you guys want to dig it up?" Richard asked. He looked to see Fiona and Bryant looking back at him with distaste? Shock?

"Are you insane?" Bryant asked.

"Yeah Richard," Fiona says, "that's just creepy."

"Well, what are we going to do now? We came out here to see the damn thing, and we have. So now what do we do?"

The three of them just stood there by that grave and thought to themselves. Bryant took out his pack of cigs and took one out. He offered smokes to Fiona and Richard. They both took one and they all shared a moment of smoke. There really was nothing to do. And it was at these moments that the reality of living within a twon high up and hidden between some mountains hit home for Bryant.

The entire evening seemed to have become one big waist. He could be at home right now with Fiona, watching a late night movie or *something*. But now he stands in a creepy wet cemetery, with thoughts about being watched.

He wanted to leave, and so he motioned for the other two to get a move on.

The walk back seemed longer than it had been getting there. Usually it is the other way around. Maybe it was the night. And the fog, covering the whole town and not allowing the three of them to see far ahead.

Nobody spoke of *her*. But they *thought* about her. It was hard not to. There was a ground rule in this town: No one was to be out after eight in the evening. Let alone after the sun went down. The reason for this was simple. The Ghost Lady. And the sheriff and town physicians were getting a little tired of dealing with the scars, broken bones, and occasional body that were turning up.

Bryant, Fiona, and Richard turned onto Maine St. and headed south, towards downtown. No one spoke, *still*. And as they passed one of many houses, Fiona happened to look over and see a woman watching them from her living room window. The woman held a cross in her hand and winced back behind her curtain as she and Fiona made eye contact.

Richard lived off of Oak St. It was another main road, running east to west, and intersecting with Maine St. From where the three of them were, the sign for Oak St. was visible. And that was where they stopped when they heard the growling coming from behind a wall of bush's.

"You guys heard that right?" Richard asked as he looked upon the green wall.

"I know I did," Fiona said as she moved closer to Bryant. "How about you?" she asks.

"Yeah, I heard it. Probably a dog. Not to worry." But he was worried. And he was trying to stay calm. To *sound* calm.

As the three of them stood there and looked, the growling started again. Only this time it was louder. And angrier. Bryany still didn't believe in the Ghost Lady. It still seemed to be a joke to him. But Fiona and Richard knew it was her. They gave each other a look. Then both looked at Bryant. He was fixed on that wall of bushes. Waiting for something to come out from behind, but nothing did. And so the three of them crossed the street. And fast.

Upon reaching the other side of the street, they heard another sound. This time they heard a howl. And Fiona was the one who turned back and looked behind them. And there she was. The Ghost Lady. Standing on the other side of that green wall.

Her eyes glowed that dark sick yellow. Her fangs showed, but were a blood red. And she grinned. As if she had gone mad.

"There she is, look," Fiona told Bryant as she grabbed his arm and turned him to see. "Look at her, Bryant. You believe us now?"

"Yeah, I believe you guys.

"I think we should get going," Richard advices and starts to walk away.

Bryant looked at Fiona. Then over at the Ghost Lady. Her eyes were the same as they had been in what he thought was a dream. And as he looked, the Ghost Lady started to walk across the street and to them. "Yeah," Bryant says and grabs Fiona's hand. "Lets get going."

The three of them walked along to Oak St. And as they walked ahead, the Ghost Lady followed. Only she didn't as much walk as she seemed to glide.

"She's right behind us!" Fiona cries out.

"Don't worry, were almost at my house," Richard says as he picks up his speed to a light run. They soon were all running. And they could still *hear* the Ghost Lady coming for them.

"AHH! HOWL! AGHH!" The Ghost Lady screams. "AHHHHHHH!"

Bryant felt a sharp pain across his back. He fell to his knees, scraping both of them. Fiona and Richard continued to head to the house. Bryant felt blood run down his back. He turned and looked to see the Ghost Lady standing over him with with her hand up to her lips. Long, bloody nails were licked clean. It made Bryant sick to see it. He even made a sound of disgust and fear. It seemed to please the Ghost Lady. For she smiled, showing those long red fangs. Her yellow eyes widened and Bryant felt more fear than he ever would again.

He tried to figure what she was. But as he did she changed form. At first she had looked human. But then her skin moved, as well as her whole figure. And she looked to take the form of a wolf. But then she would change to something else. Something that he could not make out. Something horrible. Something grotesque. As this happened (and it seemed to never stop happening), Bryant could hear the sound of her bones shifting and cracking with each form that she took. At times she would make a painful sound. And at other times, she seemed to be in extreme pleasure.

"Bryant.... RUN!" Fiona screamed from the front door. He never looked back to see if the Ghost Lady was chasing him. He just ran. Through the front yard and into the house. And from the house into Fiona's arms.

4

Bryant had received four cuts that ran from the center of his back and down. Fiona had washed and cleaned them. But just for safety measures, he went to the clinic the next morning. Richard and Fiona waited while Dr. Stevens checked him.

The story Bryant had told was that he and his friends were out in the woods and that he had lost his balance and fell into a bush. All of which caused him to end up with the scratches on his back. This story didn't, in the least bit, bring forth any sympathy from the doctor.

"You know there is a curfew that takes place everyday at the hour of eight in the evening?" Dr. Stevens asked Bryant as he applied ointment to his scars. And Bryant winced as the ointment ran over his cuts. He couldn't tell if it was because of the pain, or because the ointment was cold on his back.

"Yes, sir. I know about the rule. Its just that my friends wanted to show me something and I just couldn't say no."

"I see," Dr. Stevens said.

Bryant was lying on his stomach and looking to the left. Dr. Stevens was visible from the corner of his eye. It would have been niceto have looked at the man while the two of them were talking. The only thing in clear view was a chart on the effects of smoking. It had pictures of the human lung. From red (healthy) to black (cancer ridden). It was quite disgusting for him to look at. And so Bryant closed his eyes until Dr. Stevens placed a patch over his wounds and told him to sit back up.

"And what was it that your friends wanted to show you?"

"A grave in the cemetery."

Dr. Stevens stood by the trash and pulled off his gloves. He tossed them into the trash and washed his hands. "You know, every year some young kid, or some young couple, come into town and try to settle down here. And for a while thihgs look good but then something happens. They get stupid. Because they don't follow the rules of the town. And year after bloody year, these people are found dead outside on the streets. Or out in the woods somewhere."

Bryant only sat and listened as Dr. Stevens dried his hands. Afterwards he said to Bryant: "You look to be a bright kid, Bryant. And I, as well as the rest of the town, would love to see you stick around. So how about you do both myself, and more importantly, *yourself* a favor. Stay away from the cemetery. Stay out of the woods. And more important, obey the rules of the town. Okay?"

"I will, sir," Bryant says and puts his shirt back on.

"I saw her too," Dr. Stevens said as he took a seat in his chair. There was a brief moment of silence in the room. Bryant tried to act as if he had no idea as to what the good doctor was speaking of. Or *who*, for that matter. "You know who I am reffering to. It was during Spring break. And I had come home and was at the trunk of my car. It was rather warm as I remember it. Anyway, I had reached in to get my suitcase when someone came and stood next to me. Well, not exactly next to me. She was a few feet away. But she was there. Wearing a black dress with pale dead skin and yellow eyes. Just standing there and looking at me," Dr. Stevens tells Bryant and shakes his head in disbelief.

"What did you do?" Bryant asked.

"I ran into the house, is what I did. And I swear to you, that even now as I spek of it, that that lady was laughing as I ran away from her. Well, I got inside and slammed the door. My mother and I stood at the window and looked out into that warm night. And there she was. Looking back at us. She looked like one of those vampires that you read about in an *Anne Rice* novel. 'Come on away from the window,' my mother told me. 'She can't come inside. She is not allowed.' I never asked why that was. But I would guess that if the Ghost Lady is not aloud into someone's house without being invited, then she *is* some kind of a vampier after all. Wouldn't you say?"

"Yeah. I guess so," Bryant said as he looked at the doctor with wide eyes. He wanted to hear more but was too afraid to ask.

"I suppose that no one will ever know what she is, Bryant," Dr. Stevens told him as he opened the door. Bryant got up and walked out. But before he was to leave, the good doctor had one more thing to say. "Maybe its for the best that we don't know. As crazy as that sounds, maybe that's what keeps the Ghost Lady alive."

"That sounds alright to me sir," Bryant says.

"Yep. Sure does. Take care now."

"You too, sir."

Bryant went and wrote a check for his visit. Then he walked out with Fiona and Richard. And from that day on he obeyed the rules of the town. And he never did see the Ghost Lady again. But he could *hear* her. Late at night lying in bed with Fiona by his side. He could hear the faint sound of her howling to the night sky. Coming from deep in the woods and high up within the mountains. Awakened every night by the echoing sounds of those bells. The bells of St. Katherine.

Michael And Carolyn

1

The first letter Carolyn received came on a Saturday afternoon in mid-October. The return address said S. Marker 1, Richmond Virginia with a zip code to finish.

Dear Carolyn,

How glad I am to have built the courage to finally write you. I have been watching you for some time now. No, no. Not like that. I am no pervert. And I am in no way trying to send you a letter that would give you any discomfort. I am however writing this letter in regards to the litle crush that I have become stricken with for you. Well, I should be honest. I have more than a crush on you. I feel love for you. More love than

I think I should. But I also think that it is alright to have the feelings that I currently have.

Don't you?

Forever yours,

Michael

The first thing Carolyn did was to put the letter in her heart shaped box that her mother had given her when she was a little girl. Maybe ten years young at the time. But she really couldn't remember these days. Her childhood seemed to be only a dream to her. And she wasn't even that old yet.

Twenty eight is not forty eight by no means at all. And it has been so long since she has been with a man. Too long for that matter. But Carolyn didn't have time to sit around and think about old times. She had to get to work, pick up her paycheck, and make her weekly deposit.

The Wells is one of those trendy coffee shops that every small town, and city, has in America has these days. Carolyn had started working there last spring after she had moved in with her cousin Amber and her Aunt Katherine. It was a decision that had been talked about for a year. Carolyn had tried living on her own after her soon to be husband left her for that other woman during the holiday season. That was (without a doubt) the worst holiday season for her. But that could be said for anyone who has gone through such a bitter break-up, and at that time of year.

"We want you to come in around noon tomorrow, Carolyn," her boss, Sally, had told her as she gave Carolyn her paycheck. She has owned the shop since her husband passed away three years earlier.

Carolyn took the check and placed it in her handbag.

"Sure Sally. I'll be here. Am I still going to get those extra hours since fall is coming in?"

"Sure will, Carolyn. As many as you want. I'll see you tomorrow."

"See ya," Carolyn said and walked out the front door to The Wells and into the cool October air.

2

She had decided to keep the letter a secret. She didn't want to tell Amber or her aunt Katherine until she knew who this guy was. It was like a dirty secret. And it felt so good for her to have it. She had also decided to make a list of all possible Michael suspects that she knew and who would have written such a lovely letter. Her ex was definitely *not* on that list.

One of the things that Carolyn did to pass the time was watch movies. She had been since the break-up. And she now had a pretty good DVD collection. Her favorite was a good horror. But she also enjoyed comedies just as well. Recently, her choice of a good film was anything based on a Stephen King book. She had even gone to

New York to see the man himself on one of his book tours outside of Times Square.

On this particular night though, Carolyn decided that she would break out of her S.K. based movies, and watch Poltergeist instead. Another favorite. Ever since her childhood. She was eight when she first saw the film. She remembers not understanding it at te time. But she does remember how much she loved it. And how bad her dreams had become after seeing that clown dummy coming out from under that boys bed. Only in her dreams, it was her that was being pulled under.

She had picked up a six pack of beer, Coke, and some butter popcorn. She was all alone in the house and was in business. Aunt Katherine and Amber wouldn't be home till tomorrow. They had gone to visit their grandparents. Carolyn was asked if she wanted to go but decided that she wanted to spend the evening alone. Which was something that she hadn't had in nearly two weeks.

Carolyn had drank all but two beers, eaten a bag of buttered popcorn, and drank a can of Coke. The movie was nearly finished and she was feeling bored. So she decided to get up and get the letter that had been sent earlier.

She looked it over while sitting on her bed. It warmed her heart to receive such a nice letter from some man that she didn't even know. She knew that it hadn't come from her ex. She knew because he was too dumb to write such a lovely letter. And Carolyn wondered if (or when) she would be receiving another letter.

And she did. Three weeks later. And two days after the Thanksgiving holiday.

3

Dear Carolyn,

How I love to lay here and to think about the day that we meet. That is if a day like that could be possible. Do you think that it could be? I love to think about your long hair. I can only imagine how nice and warm it must be to become lost in.

I think often of your eyes. And how great it would be to wake up to them every morning and to see them before bed. You should write to me soon. I would love to hear from you. Share with me all the events in your life. Past and present. Tell me everything and anything.

Hope to hear from you soon.

Michael

She had received the letter on another Saturday. It seemed odd to her that the second letter should come on the same day as the first. And as lovely as this one is, it did make her feel a little uncomfortable. She wasn't sure why. It was as if the letter was tainted somehow. And there was a smell. A *stench*. She couldn't quite place it. And it was only noticeable when she held it close to her nose.

She thought the smell resembled a rotten fish. Something that had experience in knowing all about.

Her father was a devoted fisherman and had taken her on many of his trips to lakes and ponds.

Not knowing what she should write back, Carolyn decided that she should tell someone about the letter. And that someone happened to be her cousin Amber.

4

"It is so romantic," Amber told Carolyn while bouncing on the bed with excitement. Amber had been waiting since *forever* for Carolyn to get a man so the two of them coulod share details and stories with one another. "What's his name?"

"Michael. And I can't think of a thing to say to him. Matbe if I knew what he looked like, then that would give me an idea. Like: I like the way your hair is. And I like your smile. Or I love your eyes. I need help, Amber. Help me."

Now Carolyn was jumping up and down. And Amber jumped with her cousin while holding hands and laughing.

"Of course I will help you. You're my cousin. Well, your more like a sister. You know?"

"Of course I do. We are the sisters that neither one of us have ever had."

More laughing and holding hands while jumping on the bed. And after a while the two of them finally got down to business and wrote a return letter to this mysterious man named Michael.

"Oh yeah girl," Amber said. "I have to get to bed. Got school tomorrow. You know?"

"Yeah, okay. Oh my, its almost eleven. It took us three hours to write this damn thing," Carolyn says in disbelief.

"But at least it is done."

"Yeah, its done alright."

"Goodnight Carolyn."

"Goodnight."

Carolyn spent the rest of the night thinking about Michael. What he looked like. Where he lived. If he was cute or ugly. She spent the night thinking about the usual stuff.

She fell asleep watching *Salem's Lot*. Just one of her favorite movies. As well as book. And she didn't dream. Although when she had awoke, she had surely wished that she had.

5

The letter that Carolyn and Amber had written together was the best that the two of them could do. Especially after a few beers, some tequila, and tons of chocolate.

Chocolate which was much needed to help give way to the hang-over that both girls had felt the next morning.

Dear Michael,

How lovely your words are to me. You seem truly kind and I would love to possibly meet you someday. But first I need to know more about you. And I would like a picture as well. I also want to say that I hop that what I am getting into is real. I need someone to love me as I am sure you need someone to love you. I do miss having that special someone. And I hope that you could be that special man someday. I would love to have someone to talk to and spend my life with.

Sorry to keep this short. But right now I don't want to say too much. And I am also very tired. So I hope to hear from you soon. Take care.

With love,

Carolyn

The letter was sent with a two day rush delivery paid. Carolyn and Amber had both gone to the post office to send the letter. Amber had gone, not because she had nothing better to do, but because she had helped in writing the letter, and since she had taken part in it, then she was going to make sure that Carolyn fell through with mailing it.

Amber had gotten to know Carolyn a lot better since she had moved in. and if there was one thing that Amber knew about her cousin, it was that Carolyn was emotional. Just because she would say that she would do something one minute didn't mean that she would do it the next.

On the drive back home Amber says: "Damn girl! You smell like the beans you drink."

"Yes Amber. I know. Thanks *again* for telling me that."

The two of them laughed a little and in no time were pulling into the driveway.

6

Aunt Katherine leaned over the glass case at her jewelery shop and looked down at the diamond rings that filled the space there. There were two sides of the case. One was set for wedding rings. The other was for engagement rings. And Aunt Katherine leaned over the glass case and remembered the day that Bill had proposed to her. She remembered it as if it had happened only yesterday. And not fourteen years ago.

But how she wished she could live that day again. It had meant more to her than the actual wedding. Which was just as wonderful as she had always wanted it to be. But just hearing Bill ask that one question, that one question that had told her that this man was deeply in love and wanted to spend his entire life with her. It was by far the biggest compliment that Aunt Katherine had ever received.

She looked down at all those diamonds shinning their beauty into her sad eyes. She looked down at them and felt the tears run down her cheeks. She missed him.

It was three years now, and God how she missed her husband.

And why did it have to happen?

Why did the good Lord have to take her love away from her?

"Why him?" she asks quietly to herself. "Why did it have to be him?"

Aunt Katherine lowered her head and cried within the silence of that jewelry shop.

As a chilly dusk began to set in, a man in an old green Oldsmobile sat and drank a cup of coffee that he had bought earlier at The Wells. He was rather disappointed that Carolyn was not there. He hadn't seen her in quite a while. And he had really wanted to talk to her. Nothing in particular. Just the old how you doing routine.

The mans name is Steve. An old family friend. Actually, more than a friend to Aunt Katherine. She and Steve had had a *fling* back before Bill had come into the picture. And it had been Aunt Katherine who insisted that the two of them remain friends after she had broken off what they had so she could persue her interest with Bill.

And that is just one of the reasons that Steve is sitting in his car and watching as Aunt Katherine closes shop for the day. It has been nearly a year since the two of them have talked. And Steve figured that it has been long enough.

He had started waching Aunt Katherine a week ago. Following her from her shop to home. From her home to the shop. And he had even gone as far as watched (and followed) both Carolyn and Amber too. He wanted it all to go according to plan. There could be no mistakes when planning something as big as this.

It would be perfect. It had to be. And Steve figured that he, in an odd sort of way, *owed* it to Bill to take care of things since he was away.

The moon shone bright in the night sky. And the fall air had chilled down to a high thirty degrees by the time Aunt Katherine had drove out from behind the jewelery shop. She never noticed the green Oldsmobile and the man sitting inside watching her drive by.

7

"I am on my way to the store. Do you need anything before I get back?" Aunt Katherine asked her daughter.

"The only thing I need are some *supplies*. Well, that and some chocolate," Amber said.

"What kind of chocolate, dear?"

"Any. But no coconut. I hate that stuff. Yuck," Amber says and makes a gagging sound. Because it was just like she said. She hated coconut. Ever since the day she was born, she has hated it. It was the result of Aunt Katherine eating an entire coconut cake just hours before giving birth to her only child.

And now, while on the phone with her mother, Amber is once again told the story of that day so many years ago.

"I was so hungry by the time that I had bought that cake. And I myself didn't even like coconut. But whe your pregnant you find yourself eating things that you normally would never eat any other time."

"Yes mom. I know," Amber says with a long sigh. "I have heard the story about twenty times by now."

"Well now you can say you've heard it twenty *one* times. How about that my darling?"

"Great. Now I am going to go jump off the bridge. My darling." And Amber started to laugh while Aunt Katherine laughed with her. It always cheered her mothers heart to hear the sound of her daughters laugh. As it would to anyone who would ever hear it.

"Amber, I will only be a few minutes and then I'll be home. So you girls get ready for dinner. I've got a big meal planned."

"Hey mom."

"Yes."

"Isn't Patty and Sandra coming over for dinner?"

"Why yes. So we are going to have an all girl evening. Okay?"

"Alright with me," Amber assures her mother.

"I love you dear."

"I love you too, mom."

Click.

As Aunt Katherine pulled into the parking lot in front of *Krogers*, Steve pulled into the space right in front of her. He watched as she gathered her things and got out of the car, and into the store.

It was a good thing that she never noticed Steve sitting in his car. Because if she had, then she would never have gotten out of the car. Because the look of Steve's face was not one of love or compassion. It was the look of hate. And murder.

8

As the weeks came and went, more letters were written and received. And as the time came and went, Carolyn became more in love with her mysterious admirer. And the more love that she felt for Michael, the more she wanted to see him. And she had dreams. As well as paintings and poems to further indulge herself within this new love affair.

Carolyn's work at The Wells excelled. And she was given a raise as well as put full time without having to ask for the extra hours.

Everyone could see it. It was as if Carolyn's soul had been awoken after a long sleep. And her happiness made the whole world around her brighter than she could ever imagine it being.

Dear Michael,

Everyday that I awake, I think about you and wonder if today will be the day that I receive a new letter from you. I know it sounds ridiculous. But that is how I feel. I want to be with you. And I want to meet you . When can that be?

I hope that we can meet soon. You are so kind to me and I cannot wait to have you in my arms, and in my bedroom. It is so warm under the covers. And it know that if you were with me, it would be warmer.

Write to me soon my love. Lots of kisses.

Carolyn xoxoxox

And so with that letter, Michael wrote:

Dear Carolyn,

Just the thought of meeting you warms my heart. I can only dream of your touch as I lay here and think of you. I am sure that our love will be hotter than the lowest pit of Hell. And I could use a little warmth these days. It does get a triffle cold in here.

All my love,

Michael Xerox

"This whole thing between you and Michael is getting heated isn't it?" Amber asked as the two of them sat at a table in the coffee shop. She had come by to get a cup of "The finest brown beans this side of town," as she is known to say whenever she stops by.

"Yeah. We have definitely gotten closer over the past few weeks. I only hope that it stays as good as it has been going. Michael has really gotten to me. And I know that sounds ridiculous. So you don't have to give me that look okay."

And yes, Amber did have a look. A look that said Carolyn needed to come back to reality, since she apparently was way up in the clouds.

"Sorry," Amber says. "Its just that I get worried about all of this. It kinda isn't *normal.*"

"What do you mean?" Carolyn asks a bit hurt.

"Its just that you don't even know what this guy looks like. Hell, you don't even know if he even *is* a guy. It could be a woman."

"A woman!" Carolyn nearly yells. She almost laughed at Amber for even suggesting such a ridiculous idea. Carolyn didn't have a problem with the subject. Not personally. It just wasn't her thing.

"Yes, Carolyn. A woman. Or what if it just some perv that only wants to get into your pants, then drop you right after. People are like that, and the ones who *are* that way don't give a shit about anybody's feelings but there own. So just think about that. Okay?"

And even though Carolyn didn't need her cousin to lecture her on boys (especially since Amber couldn't seem to stay with a single one at a time), she knew that what Amber had told her was right. But all the same, it felt so good for her to be talking to a man again. She had truly missed it.

But still, Carolyn *did* need to be careful. Because love (even though it is one of the greatest emotions that one can ever experience), can slao be the most painful. And so Carolyn sat across from Amber and without saying a word decided that she ouwld continue to persue her love affair, and the hell with the consequences.

And it would be alright. Because Carolyn knew that it would be. No matter what Amber or anybody might say, it would be alright.

"Everything from here on out will be just fine," Carolyn told her. "Just you wait and see."

Amber just nodded her head and drank her coffee. Carolyn took a sip of hers and once again told Amber that "Everything will be just fine." But only this time, there was a hint of doubt.

The two of them enjoyed their coffee and the rest of that afternoon together in the silence that followed. While four blocks away, and sitting in his recliner in his small apartment, was Steve. He was kicked back with some beer and a small stack of photographs of Aunt Katherine. He was waiting.

9

The last letter to arrive came four days before Sunday. It was not in the least bit the usual love letter that Carolyn had been receiving. It scared her. And it made her think more about what Amber had cautioned her about weeks before.

Dear Carolyn,

How terrible I feel to write a letter like this to you. But I must. For I have seen a terrible event coming. It will happen on Sunday night. A man will come to your house and will kill your aunt and cousin. He will kill them before he comes for

you. He means to do this with a long wire. He
has dark hair and eyes. Eyes so full with rage that
it scares me to think of them. This man will wait
behind a door for his first kill. Then he will wait
under a bed for the second. And then, for the
third, he will have the lights cut off and will wait
by the front door. He will wait there because he
knows that *you* will run right for it upon finding
your loved ones in the house.

Please heed my warning. You and your family
are in great danger. The man in which intends to
come after you all is... .

And that was as far as Carolyn had read before tearing
the letter into a million pieces. She then burned those
pieces in the fireplace and had decided then that maybe
it would be best to let Michael (and all her hopes) go.

"I think that you are making the right decision about
this," Amber said over the phone. She was on her way to
Chesterfield to meet an old friend and would be gone
the entire weekend. She had just left the Richmond city
limits when she had received the call from Carolyn in
regards to the disturbing letter that had come in the mail.
"Just forget about him. Alright."

"Yeah, I know. But it was so nice to be talking to
someone again. And I... ."

"Carolyn, stop!"Amber yelled.

"What?"

"The guy is a creep. And you deserve better than
that. And besides, you still don't even know what he
looks like. Okay?"

" I know, Amber. Alright. But would you do something for me?"

"Yeah. What is it?"

"Just write this address down. And see where in the Richmond city limits this guy was writing me from."

"If I have time I will," Amber told her. Although a little annoyed with the subject. Had been for quite sometime now.

"Thank you, Amber. This really means a lot to me."

"Yeah. Whatever. But you owe me one okay?"

"Okay."

"I'll call you when I find something out."

"Alright. And thanks again."

As Amber headed into Chesterfield, Carolyn sat in her bedroom and looked over the letters she had received over the past few weeks. It made her sad to read them. She liked Michael. And now, with the thought of never talking (writing) to him again, made her want to cry. And she had come close. She felt that one tear run down her cheek, then put the letters away andf took a long hot bath.

10

Carolyn was supposed to get off work at four that Sunday afternoon. But one of the girls who worked the night shift every weekend had called and said she would be an hour late. That hour became three. And because of that,

Carolyn was late in getting home and saving her aunt from her ex-*lover* Steve.

"Come on girl. Hurry it up. Your three hours late, and now Carolyn is at overtime," Sally had told Cindy. She was more than upset. She was raging.

"Sorry, Sally," Cindy says. But the tone of her voice said something else. It said that Carolyn's hours didn't mean a thing to her. As well as showing up three hours late to the job. And she didn't last long at The Wells. No big loss.

"Whatever. Just hop on line and take over whatever Carolyn is working on."

"Yes ma'am!" Cindy yells and gets the attention of some customers. Sally sat in her office and wrote herself a note to fire Cindy whenever she can find a replacement.

Carolyn sat in her car while the engine warmed. She had the phone to her ear and was trying to reach her Aunt. The phone had rung eight times by the time that Aunt Katherine had picked answered.

"Oh hi, Carolyn," Aunt Katherine says rather cheerily. "You will never believe who is here."

"And who might that be?" Carolyn asked with a smile on her face. It was nice to hear her aunt in good spirits. She had seemed down the past few days.

"You remember my old friend Steve, don't you?"

Panic struck Carolyn's mind at the sound of his name. Yes, she remembered Steve. Aunt Katherine's old *fling*. No one had seen him for about a year now. "Dark eyes and hair," Carolyn said softly into the phone. Only

she wasn't speaking to her aunt. She was reciting a part of
the letter that Michael had sent and warned her about.

"What was that dear? What did you say?"

"Oh, it's nothing," Carolyn tells her. "Just something
I suddenly remembered."

"Alright then. See you in a few?"

"Sure."

"What's wrong Carolyn? What is it?"

"Nothing," Carolyn says in a straight forward manner.
"I have to go now. But I will see you in a little while."

"Okay. But..." And that was all that Aunt Katherine
had time to say before the line was disconnected by two
strong hands grabbing her shoulders and forcing her
onto the living room floor.

11

Carolyn's first instinct was to get on the phone with Amber
and to see if she had found anything on her mysterious
friend Michael. Her other insitinct was to ger home as
soon as possible.

"Amber, I have got to talk to you!" Carolyn says
frantically. "Something is happening over here, and I
think you should get home as soon as possible."

"Something is happening there, I don't think so.
Something is happening *here*."

"Well, what is it?" Carolyn asked rather shortly.

"That mysterious *boyfriend* that recently decided not
to talk to anymore... ."

"Yes, I know. What about him?"

"Look, don't give an attitude. I went out of my way to find out about this guy. And boy, did I find something."

"Please tell me Amber. Something really *is* happening right now. What, is he married, gay, a junkie?"

"No, Carolyn, he's dead."

"Dead. But that doesn't make any since."

"Oh, I know all about that."

"Well, how can you be so sure. Did you go to his house or apartment and knock on the door? Did you even go to the address that I gave you?"

"I am *not* going back there."

"Why? Whay the HELL NOT!"

"Because the address that you gave doesn't lead to any house or apartment. It leads to a cemetery."

There was a moment of silence. Too long. And Carolyn had to pull over to the side of the road and get her thoughts together. It just didn't make since. What she had just heard couldn't be any more true than the tooth fairy.

"A cemetery, Amber?"

"Yes, Carolyn. A goddamn cemetery. The guys name was Michael William Averall. He was young when he died. Tewnty one. He had died in some battle in the line of fire during the Civil War days. And I know it is him, Carolyn."

"And how do you know that."

"Because when I went to the cemetery to see if this is all true, and when I *did* find the headstone, there was an envelope. And it had your name on it."

A chill ran over Carolyn's body. And her skin broke out in goose flesh. This couldn't be happening. Not to her. And not now.

"This isn't possible," Carolyn kept saying to Amber. "It just can't be possible."

But it was. And the more Amber told her about how she had come about discovering the truth about Carolyn's love affair with some man whom she had never met, the more uncomfortable she felt. As well as light headed and dizzy. "This just isn't possible," Carolyn says over and over again.

But it was. And no matter how much Carolyn wanted to *not* accept what was happening, deep inside her soul, she knew that she *did*. And she knew that the letter was true. Yes, there was a man inside her home. But he wasn't hiding. He had made himself quite known to the woman with which he wanted... .

"To what?" Carolyn asks herself. "He would never do anything to hurt her. Would he?"

But something her that that was exactly what Steve was going to do. After all, he did have his heart ripped out after finding out that the woman that he had started having strong feelings for was in love with another man. But is that enough for someone to commit a crime?

"Apparently so," Carolyn tells herself. She looks down at her watch and sees that she had been sitting on the side of the road for nearly half an hour thinking things over, instead of hurrying home to make sure that her aunt was safe.

She puts the car in drive and slams on the accelerator while calling home. She was not the least bit surprised when there was no answer.

Her heart was racing. Her nerves were shot to hell. And she was sweating. She tries calling again. Still no answer. She calls the sheriffs office and makes a domestic disturbance report. She was assured that an officer was on route to the house and would be there before she got home herself.

12

"Why? Why are you doing this to me, Steve?" Aunt Katherine asked with tears running down her cheeks. "What did I do to you? Is this really happening to me?"

"Yes!" Steve shouted in her ear. "Yes it is you lying, cheating, self-centered WHORE!" He held her hands down and tied them together by the wrists. He was going to kill her. No question about it. "Just lay here and keep your damn mouth shut."

Two blocks away, a county officer was driving slowly towards the house. And coming from the other direction was Carolyn. She was closer, and had decided to approach the house even slower. She did not want to draw any attention to herself.

She had parked her car at the start of the block. She had seen the officer driving towards her, and *was* going to wait for him, but something deep in her soul told her to get a move on. And fast.

Carolyn walked slowly towards the back door, hiding in the shade of night, and got hold of the key under the back door.

13

The door lead into the basement. Which was exactly where Carolyn wanted to be. Down here she could find some kind of weapon (if needed) and she could *listen*. She still hoped that this was all just a mistake and that she was loosing her mind. Slowly but surely. *That* she could accept. If it wasn't for the sound of Steve screaming his head off at her Aunt Katherine. And the sound of her aunt crying while struggling to break free from his tight grip.

"I will kill you slow. That's what I'll do," Steve tells her. He sat on top of her with a shinning sharp knife pointing down at her stomach. "Yeah! I'll cut your insides out and make you eat them. Slowly."

"Please don't," Aunt Katherine pleaded. "Please don't hurt me. I never meant to hurt you. You and I just... Well, you know. We didn't work. And it was never supposed to be anything serious anyway. And I... ."

"SHUT THE HELL UP YOU LYING BITCH! That's all you do is lie. That's all you ever *did* was lie. So now it is my turn. Now it is Steve's turn to get a little revenge for how you made me feel."

"Please don't. I am so sorry. I'm so scared. Don't HURT ME!"

Steve pushed both his knees down on Aunt Katherine's shoulders. He tied her wrists together, placing her tied hands between her breasts. Her spine hurt. Her legs hurt. And her whole *body* was going to hurt after Steve would *lay* into her.

"Before I kill you, I just want you to know one thing. Would you like to know what that one thing is?"

"No!" Aunt Katherine answered through a heavy sob. The tears ran faster. And her eyes hurt. And Steve leaned in closer, next to her ear. One palm flat against the rug, while the other hand was made into a fist.

"I killed him."

"What?" Aunt Katherine asked with eyes wide open. The crying had stopped as well as the fear.

"Bill. Your loving husband. I *murdered* him."

"NO! NO! NO!" Aunt Katherine screams. And then *it* began.

Steve swung one hard punch to the side of her head. Stricking her ear that time. It stung bad and started bleeding. Her vision went a little blurry, but was normal in time to see the second one coming. He hit her jaw, cheeks, and every where he could find. Again and again and again. Each hit becoming *louder* than the previous one. And each hit hurting more each time received.

Steve began to choke her. And she began to gag. Her eyes rolled back and her tongue seemed to fall out from bewteen her blood stained teeth. Aunt Katherine's face turned a cherry red before a pale white. And her heart began to beat hard.

She was dying. Just like he said would happen. Slowly and painfully.

"YOU LYING, CHEATING, BITCH!" Steve screamed. His eyes were wild. The look of a man who has finally lost all control. He was in a rage. "I'LL KILL YOU! I'LL KILL Y... ."

Steve fell over Aunt Katherine, lying face down on the floor beside her as Carolyn stood over him. She held a hammer in nher hand. Cold and now bloody from that hard impact to the back of Steve's head. She stood and waited for him to make a move. *Any* move. But he never did. He was unconscious. Carolyn had fractured his skull as well as knocking him well into tomorrow.

She did not move. She was too afraid. The only sound Carolyn could hear was Steve's blood dripping off of that steel hammer as it hit the rug by her foot. She was still standing over top of him when two officers came into the house after hearing her scream for what she had done as well as what she was seeing.

15

By early spring, everything was back to normal for Amber and her mother. The trial had come and gone. As well as Steve. Locked away in a cell miles from Aunt Katherine and her daughter. But the memory was there. As well as the pain. Which was becoming less and less now since Aunt Katherine was seeing her physical therapist.

Amber was (as always) seeing as many boys as she could find them. And Carolyn was still at The Wells. Only this week, she had decided to take off to visit an old friend. A friend named Michael.

16

It was a warm, sunny, spring morning in the city of Richmond when Carolyn found his stone marker. She had decided to arrive at the cemetery early. She wanted to be alone for at least a little while before any visitors came.

There was a thick mist that covered the ground. Like a morning dew. Squirrels ran up and through the trees that grew around the many resting *homes* of the departed.

It took her awhile (close to an hour) to find him. And just as Amber had told her, there was an envelope sitting by the headstone. It was now damp and stained a light yellow. The grass was wet and had grown a bit too long and was in need of a good trimming. But Carolyn didn't mind as she sat next to his grave. She picked up the aging envelope, but before she opened it she read the inscription on the headstone. It read:

Michael William Averall

Born Aug. 19, 1842 Died Dec. 13, 1862

Killed In The Line Of Fire For The Battle Of Fredericksburg

"You were a soldier," Carolyn said. She took a sip of her coffee and placed the cup back down between her knees. She examined the envelope for a moment. Her name was written upon the front but now was barely illegeable. And for no particular reason, she ran a finger over her name to see if the ink would rub off. It didn't. She turned the envelope over and opened it. But very carefully. Inside was a single piece of paper. Neatly folded and completely dry. Much to her relief. The changing weather had not effected it at all. She read the note left for her. It read:

Dear Carolyn,

WELCOME HOME

MICHAEL XXXOOO

"Yes," Carolyn said as she placed the note down. She leaned her head against the headstone and wrapped her arms around locking her fingers together. "I am home, Michael. I'm home."

A Girl And The Skull With Roses

1

This time when he had awoke, the needle was still in his arm. He was in a daze. Sick and lucid dreaming. But he did not know what exactly he was dreaming about. All he could see were two eyes looking down upon him as they glowed a pale white. And he laid on thaat bed. And he would see those eyes. They scared him. And it sent chills down his arms and over his entire body. Which was bad for him since he still had yet to take the needle from out of his druised and bloody arm.

As soon as he moved in the slightest bit, the pain from his arm shot through him and into his stomach, causing him to curl into a ball and to try and keep from vomiting. He managed to turn over to his right side. And as he did, the needle fell out of his arm, spraying a little blood as it fell onto the bed sheets.

He laid there on his side. He figured it best if he wait till he was more awake to clean up and to *remember*. He looked at his arm. The one that had moments ago held a dirty needle. Drying blood covered the pit of his arm. And that bruise was *black*. It hurt like hell to touch. Which he continued to do for reasons that he knew not why.

It was like being in a store as a child and having to touch everything. Kinda the same thing.

Only you didn't have a goddamn needle sticking out of your arm as you walked with your parents through some store. And you weren't high. And at least you could remember what you did the night before.

Hell, he didn't even know who *he* was, let alone the ime. And so he laid there in a ball and stared at the wall. It was a dirty white. Almost yellow. And it made his stomach feel worse to look at it. So he turned onto his back and stared at the ceiling. It was worse.

There was a ceiling fan which spun around and around. And as he watched, the room seemed to spin too. He closed his eyes. He turned over onto his left side now and held his hands to his stomach. He did not want to get sick. He wouldn't. He started to shiver and gooseflesh covered his body. He could feel moisture on his forehead. He was sick. Dope sick. Only he did not know it yet.

There was a girl asleep next to him. Her name is Kimberly. At least he knew that. And his name?

Matthew Scott. He is twenty one and living with Kimberly (his girlfriend) and they have been together for?

"Jesus Christ!" Matthew shouts.

"What?" Kimberly ask's as she turned her head to look a him with her tired, dreamy eyes. Matthew was on his back again and holding his left arm. It hurt. So bad that it had caused him to shout out and wake Kimberly from her sleep.

"Screw me!"

"Again, Matthew? I would have thought that after last night you would be too tired."

He looked at her. Short, curly blonde hair with dark blue eyes. And one of the finest bodies that you would ever see. She is beautiful. And just looking at her made Matthew forget about the pain coming from his left arm.

"How long have you been awake baby?" Kimberly asked him.

He didn't know. In fact, he *still* didn't know as to what time time it was. Matthew just laid on his back and looked at her. He didn't want to speak, let alone think about anything.

Kimberly sat up. Those white bed sheets falling off of her and exposing her breasts. She reached over and grabbed her pack of Marlboro Lights from off the night stand. She then fixed her pillow and laid back lighting a cigarette quickly after. She settled both arms under her smooth white breasts. One hand holding the lit cigarette up to her lips. The other pulling the blanket and bed sheets over her legs and waist.

"How long have you been up, Matthew?" Kimberly asked again.

"I'm not sure. Ten, fifteen minutes. Maybe not even that long." Now he sat up. It hurt him all over to do it. And a strong head rush hit him, causing him to close his eyes and to think of *her*. That always made him feel so good inside.

Kimberly finished her cig and out the butt in the ashtray. She turned to Matthew and ran her hand along his chin. She laid her head against his. Matthewsarms were folded. He did not want her to see his arm or to know what had happened. She would have gotten mad and yelled. She had a temper all right. Just one of the things that Matthew couldn't stand about her. She ran her fingers over his lips and down his cheeks.

What time is it? Matthew didn't just *want* to know. He *needed* to know. He figured it to be around noon. But then remembered he owned a pocket watch and so leaned over the edge of the bed and picked his jacket up from off the floor. He reached in a pocket and pulled out the pocket watch which read: 2:58 p.m. No way he had slept that long. No way.

But he *had*. And so did she.

"How long were we asleep?" Matthew asked. And Kimberly started to laugh. So hard that tears ran down her cheeks. She was a weird one, that Kimberly Jordan. Yes, she had her moments.

"Honey," she said to Matthew after she got a hold of herself, "we were asleep for maybe five hours. Don't you remember anything?"

"No!" Matthew says sharply. He was clearly getting pissed. Kimberly sure knew how to get under his skin.

"Well, don't worry. That type of shit happens to all of us from time to time. We take too much and can't remember shit the next day. I mean, I had a night where I *banged* so much that I didn't even know my own name. That's how bad *I've* had it."

Matthew wasn't that mad anymore. Kimberly had spoken some since to him and he actually felt better knowing that she had gone through what he was going through right now.

"It happens to all of us," Kimberly said again. "Or at least I think it does," she finishes then pulls the sheets and blanket over her breasts. She then rests her head back and closes her eyes.

Silence.

Neither of them spoke for a few minutes. And while the two of them laid in silence, Matthew thought of...

He didn't know. It hurt to think. And he wanted to remember. He wanted to know what had happened the night before, and it frustrated him to not be able to remember. Or to even *think*. And so Matthew said the hell with it and went back to sleep.

2

He awoke again at 8:00 that evening. It was the sound of running water that had awoken him.

The shower.

That was it.

Kim is taking a shower.

The television was on and there was a cartoon playing on the Cartoon Network. He had no idea as to which one was plaing. All the ones that he watched came on during Adult Swim. He wanted to change the channel, but could not find the remote. And it was while looking for it that he remembered that the two of them *still* lived in that motel room. And a really messy one at that.

They were staying at the Palms Inn, in North Palm Beach, Florida. They had been staying there for two weeks now. There are two beds in the room and between them a night stand. On the night stand is (of course) a lamp accompanied by a telephone.

Clothes covered the second bed. It was a mix of his and hers. Dirty and clean. Trash was scattered over the floor. And everyday the cleaning ladies would come by and ask if Matthew and Kimberly needed a cleaning. And everyday they said no.

Matthew sat back down on the bed. Until then he had not even noticed getting out of it. And then it hit him. All at one time. He remembered. And he wanted to vomit at the same time. But he didn't. Instead his nose (of all things to have happen) began to bleed. But he didn't get himself a tissue. Instead, Matthew just laid his head back and let the blood run back into his nostril and down his throat.

He started to laugh. It was somewhat drawn. But it wa laughter none the less. And it was well needed. He was thinking that if something didn't happen soon to lighten up his spirit then he would go mad. Insane. But luckily for Matthew he found the remote and was able to keep his sanity. At least for now.

He closed his eyes and focused on the running water. It was soothing to hear. He needed that. He pulled the covers over him and thought back. Back to the night before.

He was... .

3

standing in front of a cooler in a 7-11. He was looking for something to drink. Kimberly was getting a grape soda. They both wanted to get really drunk and Kimberly had told him to get some Miller High Life.

He hated it.

But then, Matthew would do anything for his girl since after all that was what Kimberly *now* was. He would even kill for her (if need be) because that is just how he is.

But right now Matthew wants to drink wine. But all the store has is red. And he hates the red. It always makes him sick. So instead he bought some Budweiser for him and that Miller brand for her.

The 7-11 that they were in stood at the entrance of the Inn that they were staying. A rather convenient store to have around while staying (living) in a motel. And it was while standing at the counter and paying for their supplies that Mattew remembered the night that the two of them had met.

It was a Saturday night in a bar at City Place. That renovated place in downtown West Palm Beach. Matthew was sitting alone and drinking beer. He had been there for nearly an hour when someone had fell aganst him from behind. He had heard some commotion but didn't bother to turn and see what was happening. It was nothing serious. It had been Kimberly and her friend Sarah Blackwell acting loud and making fools of themselves.

Matthew was working on his fourth beer when Kimberly had ran into him, causing him to spill his beer over his shirt and lap. He wasn't exactly angry. *Keep it cool*, he told himself. And he turned to look at the person who had caused a break in his drinking.

He surely didn't expect to see a curely blonde haired beauty smiling drunkenly at him with her soft pink lips and dark blue eyes. But that is just what he was seeing.

She apologized and introduced herself. Matthew had told her that he was pleased to meet her and that "all was good." He ordered another beer for himself and one for her. He got up off of the bar stool so that she could sit down. His crotch was wet and it *did* bother him. But he did his best to dismiss it. And after a few minutes talking to Kimberly, he did.

And then Kimberly would do something that would come back to haunt her. Very hard. She introduced her friend, Sarah Blackwell, to Matthew Scott. And like I just said, it would be a mistake that she would not be able to live down for quite some time.

"I am pleased to meet you, Matthew."

"The pleasure is all mine, Sarah."

And as the two of them shook hands, Kimberly turned away from them and took a sip of her beer. And at that moment, that handshake turned into holding hands and running each others fingers over the others. If only for a moment. But it was enough. And then Sarah said goodbye and was gone.

Matthew felt his soul ache as he watched her go. Kimberly didn't pay any mind to her friend leaving. She was too drunk to care. She and Matthew stayed at the bar for a while longer before going to her apartment. Kimberly was, at that time, staying with some other girls with whom attended classes with her at Florida State University. They had all gotten an apartment between the West Palm Beach and Palm Beach Gardens city limits.

Matthew and Kimberly had spent the rest of that night engaging in hard, loud sex. So loud that the next morning Kimberly's roommates had kicked her out. She was quickly replaced. And no one had missed her.

"It was building up. The tension between me and my roomies that is," she had told Matthew later on that day.

And so the had stayed at his place for two months. Matthew had a place in a trailer park. Not a trailer, but a small house just at the entrance of the park. He had two roommates with whom he never spoke to. He would see them from time to time. But only outside when they were coming or going. It really was a small house and the landlord had warned him about having someone else stay with him. It was forbidden. And it would be grounds for eviction. A stupid rule. But it was one no less. And luckily for them, the landlord did not stay anywhere near the house. So that gave Matthew and Kimberly th extra time that they would need to save for when they did get kicked out from there.

The room was small. Too small for two people. Take two steps once inside and you ru into the bed. Take one step to the right and you met the wall. But it worked considering the circumstances at the time. All Matthew and Kimberly did there was eat, sleep, and have sex.

And when it was time to go, they had made a home at the Palms Inn Motel. And that is where they have been staying since. What did I say, two weeks now?

4

He paid the clerk and they walked out of the 7-11 and back to their room. There room was on the second floor and was room number 310. Matthew could never figure why that mattered so much to him. It just did.

They put the snacks away and opened two cans of beer. The television was always on and The Simpsons was playing. It was a re-run. As always. And while the show played Kimberly and Matthew had a long discussion about the show.

"The show is genius, but weird at the sme time," Kimberly states.

"I think it's the greatest thing to happen to television. As well as myself," Matthew tells her proudly. He is, without a doubt, a very dedicated Simpson fan. "We really need a DVD player. Maybe we can seel some of the shit that we bought and get a cheap one. Blockbuster up in Jupiter has some for real cheap. And I need to go up there tomorrow anyway to see someone."

"Who?" Kimberly asked.

"Just some friends I haven't seen in a while."

"Okay. Sure. Why not," Kmberly says. But there was uncertainty in her voice. Matthew heard it and loved it.

As big as a bitch that Kimberly could be, it made him happy to know that he could make her worry.

There were no friends.

Just Sarah.

Matthew had seen her at his work a few nights before. She had came in with one of her friends who attended the university with her. That girls name is Carmen. A black girl who had come down from Chicago to attend (and graduate) in business.

She and Sarah had one class together and had always been close. Even on that first day of class. And now they sat and watched Matthew as he worked in a small pizza restaurant in Lake Park. He was on salary and there quite a lot.

The first second that he had a break, he had gone and sat with Sarah and her friend Carmen. And they had made plans to meet. But then he had awoken the next day with a needle sticking out of his arm, dope sick coming off heroin, and forgetting about his plans to meet Sarah.

And now he is laid out on the bed covered with bed sheets and thinking: *Your screwed now. Sarah will kill you for this shit.*

Well, at least he didn't have to work this day. It was a Wednesday. And it was now nearing half past eight this fine evening.

Kimberly came out of the shower and laid next to him. She placed her head on his chest. *Thank god for the towel around her wet hair.* It was warm on him as well as her body. And Matthew became aroused by the feel of her and so removed the towel which covered her smooth body.

Then he was inside her.

No foreplay. No sweet talk. Straight in. They had sex a lot. No matter what the mood. And no matter how high or drunk the two of them got, they had sex. It was, in a way, the one thing that kept them together. And it was good. Oh, so good. He loved the feel of her. Maybe not as much as with other girls he had been with. But with Kimberly? Yes.

So warm, he thought as he was inside her. *So warm.*

5

He sat up and pulled a pillow behind his back. He leaned back and looked at the remote. It was too big and dirty. Really dirty. He laid there and looked at it for a moment. It was just so ugly. He picked it up then set it on the night stand. He then looked at his left arm. The blood was still there. Dried and scabbed around the hole from where the needle stuck out from earlier.

And the sheets. Even the sheets were stained with his blood.

He picked up the remote again and turned up the television. The news was on and there was a coverage going on for the up and coming hurricane season. Tips on what to buy. What to overstock on. And tips on where to go if things got a bit *ruff*.

Kimberly had gone to the bathroom to clean herself off. She always did after. And Matthew was about to get up and go in as well when she came out.

"I was just going to get up and go in," he said to her as she walked over to his side of the bed. "My arm is a mess. Look at it."

She was wearing a towel around her waist. That was all she had on and that was the way that Matthew liked it. She sat down next to him. "Aw, baby. Let me see."

"Here you go nurse. Do you think you can help me?"

She grabbed his left hand and pulled his arm out towards her. She studied the dried blood before pulling his wrist close to her lips. There was the tinnitest bit of dried blood there. She covered the area with her lips and ran her tongue over it. She licked her way from his left wrist to the pit of his left arm.

"Mm, mm, mm. You taste so good, Matthew."

"Well, that's good to know," he replied.

Blood covered her lips and tongue. It was so wet and thick. And she had started off slow and easy. But by the time her lips had touched that scab, she was licking and sucking hard. And it hurt Matthew. And he winced from the pain. He even felt sick as he felt that scab reopen and tear from his skin. And it hurt as the blood was sucked out of his bruised vein.

He couldn't take anymore. He placed his hand under her chin and pulled her head up toward him. Her eyes were dazed and dreamy. He leaned over and kissed her. The taste of blood was immediate in his mouth. Matthew couldn't think of the word to describe the taste. But it always reminded him of the taste of an old and used penny.

Matthew pulled Kimberly close to him and removed the towel from around her waist. He ran his hands over the back of her body and pulled her on top of him. He leaned back.

So warm, he thought again.

So warm.

About an hour had passed when they had finished having sex. Some people would call it making *love*. But what Kimberly and Matthew did could hardly be considered as anything close to love.

They were both *dirty* and needed a shower. This would be Kimberly's second and Matthew's first for the day. The bathroom was standard size, with the exception of the shower. It was made for one. And as a result of the limited space, there was a bit more sex to be had.

It wasn't as long this time. And it was somewhat uncomfortable for the both of them. So they finished, let the water run off the soap from their bodies, dried off, and ran back into the bed. It was just too damn cold for the both of them. The A/C was always running and always set on 65 degrees.

No more sex would happen that night. They wanted to ride that train. So after a few minutes the two of them got dressed. Kimberly went to the table which sat in a corner at the end of the second bed and by the porch door.

There were some magazines scattered with cigarette butts and ashes spread over them. There were used and un-used matches. A spoon used for cooking. A syringe (the same one of which was sticking out of Matthew's arm when he had awoken hours before) and two packets, made from folded foil, which contained a dark brown powder inside.

"Come here. I am fixing yours first," Kimberly tells Matthew.

He was slow to move. He, in fact, didn't even want to get up. And so Kimberly called him again. Only this time with some obvious fustration. She really could be a bitch sometimes.

6

"Matthew, come HERE!" Kimberly shouted.

Matthew didn't want an argument. So he did the sensible thing and got up and went to her. He sat next to her at the table and laid his left arm over the scattered magazines. Kimberly took a tie and wrapped it above the bruised vein. She watched in a sick excitement as the vein grew bigger. She gave matthew the syringe and watched him *bang* his fix.

Matthew had made sure to stick the needle above the bruise. A shot of blood ran into the tube. And with that one quick push, it was gone. He then placed the syringe on the table and went back to the bed and laid back down.

Kimberly fixed herself up shortly after. She had cooked up more than she should have for herself. She was becoming addicted.

7

Matthew Scott was born in Orange County, California and was brought into this world and into the arms of an Irish family. His mother Katherine and father Peter were more than overjoyed with the new arrival.

He is their third child and the only son that his mother and father would have. They would have njo more children after Matthew was born. Three was more than they could handle.

Peter was a marine and was on a four year plan with the option of going on longer and making a career in the service. Which he did. And which he then decided to move his family out of the coastal west, and into the state of Virginia.

Matthew had just turned three then. His two older sisters were eight and five. His eldest sister, Jenna, tended to demand more attention than the second eldest, Andrea. Whith whom was a very happy child. Always smiling and wanting to laugh. Matthew, at that time (and even now), was cool and relaxed.

When he was three his hair was long and blonde. His mother never wanted to cut it. She loved it too much. And now at the newly age of twenty one, his hair is a dark brown. Not long, but growing.

He had moved down to West Palm Beach, Florida for two reasons. One: to get away from the small town life that Virginia has all too much to offer. But there was also another reason. And two: he was attending school. Well, trying to. He spent more time partying and falling in with any girl he could find. And then there was the ocean. He loved the water just as much as the woman.

And they loved him back too. At times, *almost* more than he could handle. But it was always good. And he loved the attention. Plus the company. And it was even better when his ex would come down for a 'friendly' visit. Didn't happen too often. But always at the right time.

Matthew got around. But not so much as to build up a reputation. He made sure of that. But through it all, Matthew just wanted that one girl. That one love that would consume and dominate him like no other could.

He would sometimes find himself alone at the beach late at night and would think about *her*. Thinking about how nice it would be to have someone who would stay and never want to leave. He could get so lonely at times. And so he would sit on the beach at night and look at the stars and the moon as they lit up that dark sky.

He would sit there alone and listen to the waves come in and would drift away into his thoughts as the breeze, always so nice and warm as it ran across his face, came running by.

He missed those nights. And it has been a long time since he has had the time to himself to go back and experience them. Having Kimberly as a girlfriend meant having to give up a *lot* of your free time.

And now his time with her is spent high on *train* and watching her take the same syringe that he had just used on himself and stick it into her vein as it pulses in her thin pale arm. And now Kimberly is lying next to him on the bed and fading out into her own world.

"Goddamn right!" Kimberly yelled out. She had been lying there next to him and had seemed to have been sleeping when she suddenly yelled out while sitting up and leaning back against the headboard. "This is some grade A shit right here. What do you think?"

"I think I want to go to the beach," Matthew says as he scratches at his arm.

Kimberly lit a cigarette.

It was a Camel.

But she only smokes Marlboro Lights. So where did these come from? What is she up to? What has she been doing?

Matthew also noticed a small piece of paper that held someone's phone number on it. It was stuck between the cigerette box and the plastic cover that it sits in. Matthew started to get that feeling from deep down. The feling that something wasn't right. That there was something going on whiloe he was away.

Possibly while she is at work. Someone that she works with. You know that it is not som,eone from the lot. Because when you are here she is here.

He sat up hiself and leaned back. *Then forget the whole mess and go to the beach. And by the way, who the hell are you to get so defensive over something when you had made plans to go meet her friend , Sarah, earlier today? Get over it man.*

And he did. For now at least.

"Well, I am all for going to the beach. Whenever you are ready, my darling."

"I need to get dressed in something warmer. And so do you, Kim."

"Oh piss off, Matthew. I'll go naked if I want to and you'll just have to deal with it."

Kimberly was starting to act up again. Matthew couldn't figure what it was, but whenever Kimberly banged up, she acted as if she were too good for him.

Let alone anyone else. She was, in all thruth, acting like a bitch.

About the only thing she will ever be good at, Matthew thought as he watched her dance around the bed. Swinging her arms as she talked non-sense to him even though he didn't even bother to listen. She was really acting the part of an upper class snob.

Stupid bitch.

Matthew got up and off the bed, got dressed, and put on his jacket. He picked up his wallet and car keys to his PT Cruiser. He was hoping that Kimberly would see this, shut her mouth, and would follow what he was diong. And he was right. She had stopped talking and acting stupid as soon as he had reached for his keys.

It didn't take her long to get ready. She was too high to care for how she looked. And that was just the way Matthew liked it. He,of course, liked his girls to look nice for him. But at the same time, he couldn't stand it when (for example) Kimberly would spend fifteen minutes trying on dofferent things and asking the same damn question over and over again.

"How does this look?" "

"How does my hair look?"

And then there were the clothes that she didn't *feel* right in. But every guy goes through that in a relationship. Some not as bad as others. This was the worst. And Kimberly was the worst at it, and it was at these times that she would get into one of her moods and would yell at him and at *anything* else around her if she couldn't find just one particular thing to focus her anger on.

But never mind that her clothes were in a massive pile that started on the second bed and finished on the already littered floor.

But now they are in his PT Cruiser, cruising up route one (northbound) heading into Juno Beach. He took a right turn and was driving on Ocean Blvd. On the right there are condominiums and apartments with parking lots between them.Free to all who know where to find them. And from there, access to the beach.

There is a beach house which sits between two paths. Both take you to the beach. The one on the right has a deck that most of the locals hang around. That was the path that they took. And as Kimberly and Matthew passed by, they never noticed Sarah Blackwell sitting with her boyfriend and one of her roommates having some of their own fun. They were all drinking. Had been for a while.

Sarah's boyfriend, Chris, lived in an apartment there and had parties every weekend. The three of them had taken a leave from the party to get some air and relax from the crowded rooms of the apartment that Chris and his two roommates, Brian and Steve, shared.

Sarah sat next to her roomy Jen. They both listened to Chris talk drunkenly about his car and a bunch of other things that really didn't interest her, or Jen, in the least bit. The only reason that Sarah was with him was because of the parties that he held. It was quite the scene for her and some of the other students at the university. Sarah couldn't stand him. She thougt that he was one of the dumbest persons she had ever known.

"Sarah!" Chris called to her. He had noticed that she was not paying any attention to what he was saying.

She had placed her attention on the couple that had just walked by. "Pay attention when I speak. Okay?"

Sarah turned to look at Chris, and as she did, Matthew turned to look back at the three people sitting at the deck. He wasn't sure, but he swore that he heard the name Sarah being called out. And of course, when he looked he *did* see one blonde haired girl sitting next to a brunette.And it could be her. But how was he to tell from where he was standing. And besides, her back was to him.

They were walking now. Both of their shoes had been left at the end of the path. Or maybe it was the beginning. All depends on how you look at it.

They stopped and sat down right at the touch of the evening tide. The water ran warm across their feet. The moon was full and the night sky was filled with a million stars. These were the moments that Matthew missed. It was at times like these that everything went away and he could be at complete peace with the world. Just him and the sound of those waves coming in fom that open sea.

He thought about it while high from the heroin that he had *banged* and while sitting next to a girl that he really didn't want to be with. A girl who started to laugh and rock back and forth, holding her arms around her shins, and placing her chin on her knees.

"Wow. Ha, ha, ha, ha, ha," Kimberly laughed loudly. She continued to do this for a while. Matthew tried to get back to his happy thought, but Kimberly kept breaking it with her obscene laughter. "Ha, ha, ha, ha, HA!" she laughed in his ear. She wanted to piss him off.

God, I hate you, Matthew thought as he looked at her with his dark eyes. Back and forth she went. And then she fell over and onto him. Her head in his lap. *At least she stopped laughing. And at least now I can... .*

Something out of the corner of his eye. Matthew turned to look and saw a girl standing there. She was looking at both of them. Looking at them was anger and disgust. She was wearing jeans and a white tank-top. Her hair was long and a dirty blonde. It fell over her shoulders and moved with the evening breeze.

Its her. Its Sarah.

His heart filled with a happiness that he never thought he could ever feel. And it must have shown on his face, because at that moment, Sarah gave him a smile. And then she turned and went back up the path and to the deck.

And that was all there could be for Matthew and Sarah.

For now at least.

Matthew and Kimberly sat at the beach for nearly an hour. When the two of them decided to leave, their high was still going strong, but now they were hungry and wanted to eat.

8

Kimberly walked ahead of Matthew. Neither of them said much. They were both feeling tired and out of it. They stopped at the deck to sit and put on their shoes. As they did, Matthew caught a glimpse of a writing on the seat of the wooden bench from which he now sat. It just happened to be the same seat of which Sarah had sat. Kimberly had her shoes on and started to walk to the Cruiser.

"Hurry up, Matthew," she demanded coldly.

"I will be there when I get there!" Mathew shouted back at her. That feeling of anger was building inside him again. He wanted to scream. *But you can't. You can't loose your cool.* His shoes were on and he stood up. But before he left he looked at the writing on the seat of the bench. And what he saw excited him as well as put him in a daze. It made him want *her* here and now. It made him want to tell Kimberly to go to hell and go to *her* and make *her* go away with him.

And he knew, more than ever, that the two of them would be together. And he wanted it to be right then. Right... NOW.

What Matthew saw was a heart drawn from a black marker. And within the heart were two names. Sarah and Matthew.

9

On the way back to the motel, they smoked a bowl of marijuana. It was a nice high. Just what the two of them needed. But what it really did was make them so very hungry. And in Matthew's case, really thirsty.

There are always plenty of Palm Beach police parked along Route 1 late at night. And because of this well known fact, Matthew and Kimberly had decided to walk to the diner from their motel room. It was a good two miles. Which doesn't sound so bad for most people. But, if you have ever taken drugs before, then you would know that the last thing one would want to do especially after taken a good quantity of *stuff* (which ever it may be) is to walk anywhere.

But they did. And the weather was nice and warm. And the night sky was just as clear as it was on the beach. The moon was full and bright. And it had that ring around it. That ring which Matthew could never remember the name. But it always reminded him of an eye. A great big eye that looked down upon all of us.

The eye of God, he had once thought. Even though he doesn't have such faith in the idea of a god. But he always figured that if there *is* a god, that that would be a good way for him (or her) to look down and watch all the people on his (or hers) planet.

But now it is time to forget such nonsense and go inside the diner with his girlfriend and eat a bunch of junk that the two of them really don't need.

When they had gotten back to the motel, they *banged* one up again. Only more this time. And so the high was much better. There was no breeze from the ocean. There was no walking. Hell, there was no talking. Which did them both just fine. They laid on the bed, watched television, and faded into the night. And for Matthew that all too familiar itching felt better than ever before.

Twenty miles north was the restaurant that Kimberly worked at. It sat just outside the Jupiter town limits. She had to be ther at nine the following morning. And after

the night that she and Matthew had, Kimberly was in no
condition to work. And as always, whenever she felt sick,
tired, or down, she took out her misery on Matthew.

"Damn, I am going to be late again. Why didn't you
get me up earlier?" Kimberly yelled. She had told him
before falling asleep to get her up at exactly 8:30. And
because she was too lazy to get up, she will be late for
work. She has only been working for two weeks. She
didn't have a car, so Matthew gave her a ride everyday
that she needed to be there. He did this with no fuss
and with a happy heart. He enjoyed the drive (well, the
drive that came after dropping Kimberly off at work),
and would drive back, windows sown, radio turned loud,
and just taking in the scene. Girls in bikinis. Lying on
the beach, Walking the dog. Roller-skating on that long
sidewalk while surfers hit the waves. The ocean water so
blue that at times Matthew couldn't tell where the water
ended and the sky began. The sand so white. And the
weather so warm. He was at peace again. These drives
alone was like sitting on the beach alone late into the
night. All those nights to himself so many weeks ago. He
wanted them back. He *needed* them back. He...

Was standing by the door to the motel room,
patiently, while Kimberly yelled at him for washing her
clothes and not folding them. She had asked if he would
have them washed when he did his laundry. And she
herself never folded her own clothes (or his) when she
washed them.

"This is bullshit. Can't you ever think of me and my
comfort? You are so self-centered." Then finally: "Grow
up."

Kimberly said these things as she put on her waitress uniform. Then she fixed her hair. Which took too long to do. I mean, how long does it take to put hair into a ponytail? Not more than five minutes I can tell you. But with Kimberly...

It was twenty after nine that morning when Matthew dropped her off at work. Kimberly had bitched the wole drive up. She bitched about being hungry. She bitched about needing her coffee. And she bitched about a whole bunch of other things that Matthew ignored. He was thinking about Sarah. He had decided that he would try and see her after dropping Kimberly off. He knew the number. Kimberly had made the mistake of storing it as a *friends* contact on her cell phone.

He pulled in front of the building of her work. He wanted Kimberly gone. It was official (or at least it was in his mind), he was done with Kimberly Salt. That was as long as things with Sarah went well. And deep within Matthew's heart, he knew that it was good. So very good.

"See you later, Matthew," Kimberly said rather sharply as she opened the passenger side door. She didn't even look at him. And she slammed the car door after she got out. And that was one thing that Matthew had told her not to do before. It had always bothered him. And she clearly had done it thid time to piss him off.

"Worthless whore," Matthew yelled out as he drove off. He didn't even check to see if she had turned around sfter hearing him. He didn't even know if she *had* heard him. Matthew didn't even care.

Matthew drove west on Indiantown road and Parked in a Wendy's parking lot. He didn't own a cell phone himself, so he had to use the payhone. He thought that he must look to others as a junkie calling for his fix. He knew he looked used up. But as long as he thought of Sarah nothing mattered.

He needed to eat. He didn't realize ust how hungry he was until he had dialed Sarah's number. His hands were shaking a little, and it made it a bit uneasy when dialing the number. But he had the idea that after he hung up the phone (after a call that he hoped would be a good one) that he would get some breakfast from the Wendy's restaurant. He had never really cared for breakfast, it never made him feel too good after eating any kind of it.

"Matthew?" Sarah asked with a touch of excitement in her voice.

"Yeah, its me, Sarah. I was thinking that since I am in the area that maybe we could meet up. What do you say?"

"Yes. I would really like that, Matthew. I was beginning to think that you didn't like me since you never showed up the other day," Sarah says. She then took a bite and began to chew rather loudly into the phone. It sounded as if she had bit into an apple. And the sound of her eating made Matthew think more about the hunger that has overcome him. "So I guess wse should make a plan to meet somewhere then , huh?" Sarah asked while eating her food.

"Well, I am at a payphone in the Wendy's parking lot. Can you meet me here or would you rather have me meet you? Its whatever you want, Sarah."

"That's alright. I can come and meet you there. I *do* really need to talk to you, Matthew." Sarah's voice took a more serious tone. "There is something you should know. And I guess this morning would be a good time as any. Or I should say that this *is* the best time."

She took another bite. Matthew knew that it was an apple this time, but asked anyway.

"Are you chewing on a piece of an apple, Sarah?"

"Yep."

"Is it the green kind or the red?"

"Green of course. Those are the best."

There was a brief moment of silence. But it was good. For Matthew could feel it. He could have held that phone all morning and day, listening to Sarah talk and eat green apples. The world seemed a lot nicer listening to her breathe.

"Well then, Matthew. I am going to hang-up and get myself ready, and I will be over to see you just as soon as I can get there. But just to make sure, you are at the Wendy's on the corner of Indiantown road and Military Trail, right?"

"Yeah. Just look for a grey PT Cruiser sitting in front of the payphone."

"I will, baby. I can't wait to see you."

"I can't wait to see *you*, Sarah. Get here fast, ok."

"I will."

Click.

And so Matthew hung the phone back up, went into Wendy's, and ordered an egg and sausage biscuit with a Coke. It tasted horrible and the soda was too sweet. But it did take care of the hunger problem.

Sarah arrived fifteen minutes after they had talked and pulled her car in right next to his PT Cruiser. She was driving a red BMW convertible, and had insisted that he get in and that they go for a ride. Matthew did this with not a problem in the world.

They went to the beach. Juno beach to be exact. Sarah parked her car in the front of the parking lot where her now ex-boyfriends apartment was, and where the night before she had seen Matthew and Kimberly sitting in the moon lit dark.

As the two walked to the beach, Sarah asked if Matthew liked the message that she had left for him. The fact that she would even *know* that he would have seen it excited him even more.

"Very much," Matthew said to her as they both looked into each others eyes. They had stopped just past the very bench of which had become the topic in conversation. Matthew had wanted to ask how she had known that he would see the *love* note, but thought it best to just keep things the way they were.

Nothing was said and the only sound was the distant crash of the morning waves. Then Sarah smiled. She took Matthews hand and said "lets go."

They sat on the warm sand a few feet from the running water. The cold Atlantic just barely touching their feet. A slight breeze came in and Matthew felt again the peace that he had missed. They sat close to each other. As close as two people possibly can. Matthew could not stop looking at her. She wore a white tank top with old worn blue jeans. Her hair is long and looked almost golden in the sunlight.

She closed her eyes as the breeze blew across her smooth face. And Matthew felt love for her. Deep and strong. Sarah opened her eyes and looked at him. She was smiling and her eyes (a dark green that seemed to shine like an emerald) made his heart melt. Matthew moved in to kiss her and she placed her hand on his shoulder and stopped him. She clearly did not want to kiss him. And he wanted her. He wanted her more than he should have.

Matthew didn't know what to do next. He couldn't just sit there after making a fool of himself. And that was just how he felt.

"Its okay, Matthew. I want you too. But it can't be now. Not when you are still seeing *her*, and if you were to kiss me then you would be cheating. And if you cheat on her, then I don't think, or in fact, I *know*, that I wouldn't be able to trust you."

Matthew had sat back and listened to her every word. Sarah had taken her hand off his shoulder and was now holding his hand. It felt so good to him. They both ran their fingers over the others. And at times they would hold tight. And at other times it was gentle.

"I broke up with Chris, and I want you to know that I did it for you," Sarah told him as he looked at her. He was about to speak when she stopped him. "I know that this may sound crazy, but its *you*, Matthew. And it has always been. Ever since the first night that we met I knew it. And I know tou do too. And so I am telling you that enable for you to be with me, you *have* to leave ber. There is no other way. But that is just plain common knowledge. You know?"

Matthew had said that he understood. And Sarah told him that as soon as he and Kimberly were through, that all the feelings that the two of them had for each other would bloom into a world of true love, and that they would be one, and that no person would ever come between them.

"I will do it today," Matthew tells her. "I'll do it *now* if it pleases you."

"No, Matthew."

This took him by surprise. Sarah let go of his hand and brushed his hair away from his face. She looked at him with some of the true love that she had spoken of minutes before. Then says to him, "Do it because you *want* to and because you *want* me."

"Allright, Sarah."

And then that was all there was for a few minutes. They both sat side by side and took in the morning together. They held hands and Sarah leaned her head on his shoulder. The two of them would never say it to anyone (let alone to each other), but neither one of them would ever want this one time together to ever end.

They sat in silence and enjoyed the time they had together. Matthew was once again at peace and did not want it to end.

"You need an boyfriend, Sarah?" Matthew asked as she turned her eyes up towards his.

"Depends. You looking for a girlfriend?"

They sat in Juno Beach until Sarah had to get to class. In the Wendy's parking lot they gave each other a long and emotional hug.

10

That night Matthew was alone. Kimberly had not been at her work when he went by to get her. And when Matthew had gone inside and asked for her, two of the waitresses looked at each other and acted as if they were hiding something. *What do they know?* Matthew thought as he stood at the front door of the restaurant. *Where is Kimberly?*

One of the waitresses, a chubby redhead with black eyeliner and black fingernail polish, told Matthew that Kimberly had left early. Around quarter past nine, she had said. The restaurant closed at eleven every night, and since Matthew didn't know what to say (or what else to ask) he decided to leave. But before he would leave, one of the waitresses would tell him that she was sorry. *Sorry for what?*

Once outside, Matthew got back in his Cruiser and went back to the Inn.

He drank beer and watched some crappy sitcom. He wanted to call Sarah. He wanted to be woth her and to forget all about Kimberly. And as he laid on the bed, he knew that she was with someone else. He was no dummy. And he also knew that Kimberly would try and give him some bullshit excuse for not being there with him. But it was okay. He knew what she would do and he would not accept anything that would have to say. It was over. For he belonged to Sarah now. *If only that stupid girlfriend of mine were here for me to tell her*, Matthew thought and smiled. For he would have to opportunity to tell her soon enough. The next morning was coming fast. And it would be a morning that Kimberly Salt would live to forget.

As Matthew was lying on the bed and thinking about Sarah, Kimberly was lying in the bed of one of the waiters with whom worked with her. His name is Jeff. One of those all American self-centered jack-asses. He thought he was the man. A know it all. And always in everybodies business, thinking for himself first before others, looking a lot *prettier* than a man should.

He laid on his bed, next to Kimberly, and lit a Camel cigarette. He took a good long drag. Then he passed it on to Kimberly as she pulled the covers over her breasts. She was hot and sticky was drying sweat.

"He's so stupid and he doesn't know anything. He is so messed up on *junk* I am surprised that he even knows his own name anymore," Kimberly says angrily. Jeff just listened. He couldn't give a spit for Matthew's life or what he was *on*. Jeff (truth be told) really didn't care all that much for Kimberly. She was just a good time for him. And she wasn't even all that good. There were plenty of other girls waiting in line to get with him. He wasn't a bad looking guy. Looked like the type one would see modeling in some magazine or catalog. But it was his attitude. And that eventually killed his appeal with the ladies and friends. Which is why he goes through so many.

The next morning Kimberly had to take a cab back to the Inn. Mathew was in the shower when she had come into the room tired and hung-over. She never realized the dark purple hickey on the side of her neck. Kimberly felt dizzy and wanted to be sick.

"Where were you?" Matthew asked Kimberly as she laid on the bed. She wouldn't give an answer. All she *would* do is look upon him with disgust. And what did she have to be disgusted with? Matthew paid for her to have a place to stay. He drove her everywhere. He... I think I have already covered earlier what Matthew has done for her. But just for the record, matthew would make damn sure that *she* would know.

"Oh shut the hell up!" Kimberly screamed and sat up on the bed. "You never think about anyone but yourself. And I..."

"I am done with you, Kimberly," Matthews says rather calmly. She sat, stunned after what she has just heard. Kimberly's eyes are wide and she doesn't even know how to respond to what Matthew has told her. It is a miracle. Kimberly speechless. It was one of the greatest moments that Matthew would ever have while being with her. "I have found someone else," Matthew tells her. "I think you know her. But I am not going to tell you who she is, because ei am more than certain that you will find that out in time."

Matthew felt good and telling Kimberly this (as well as other things but they shall be left out), put him on a natural high that only comes once in a blue moon. He loved it and he loved leaving Kimberly speechless.

"I HATE YOU!" Kimberly screams and charges for him. Before Matthew could have time to think on how to react, Kimberly pushes him. Matthew stayed cool (as always) even though wanted to push her back. "I ope you know that I messed around behind your back. I get it real good from this guy who actually cares about me,"

Kimberly says while shaking her fist at him. "So, burn in HELL!"

"Is that all you have to say?" Matthew asked.

"At the moment that *is* all I am going to say. I'll talk to you later, Matthew. Obviously uou have stuff that you need to do and so I suggest that you get the *hell* out of my face and do them."

And that was it. That was the end of Matthew and Kimberly. Matthew left and came back seven hours later. He had planned it just right so that he could go back to the room after Kimberly had left for work. That was also depending on *if* she had even left. But Matthew had had a plan for *that* if the situation had arose.

Matthew had walked out and got into his Cruiser. First thing that he did was take a long drive. He went south to West Palm Beach and had gotten off the interstate when arriving at the Palm Beach Lakes Boulevard exit. He drove east and stopped at a gas station and made a call. Matthew was feeling pretty good. And since he was out with the old and in with the new, he decided to treat himself to a little fun.

"Joe?" Matthew asked after a voice answered his call. It had been a while and Matthew wasn't sure at first if he had contacted the right person.

"Yeah, this is Joe," a man answered.

"Hey man, its Matt. Wanted to know if you had any train tickets for sell?"

"Well lets see, I think I have some for your skinny ass."

"Cool man. I'll be right over..."

"No man. Cops been watching the neighborhood. Its *hot*, you know? How's bout I meet up wit you." This was in no way a question and Matthew knew it all too well.

"Okay. Meet me in the front parking lot of the mall. Just look for my grey Cruiser and me, of course."

"Allright. Give me ten."

Matthew hung up the payphone and got back in the car. He drove not even half a mile to the entrance to the mall.

He parked.

He waited.

Joe (if that was his real name) was a well known heroin dealer for those *lost* within that high. He had been selling for twenty two years and had only been caught once. He was good. But even the best slip up from time to time. He pulled up besides Matthews PT Cruiser in a black van. Matthew could never tell what year (or make) the van was. And he never bothred to ask. Joe was not the type of guy that Matthew really wanted to get to know on a personal level. And he wasn't even that old of a guy. Thirty five but looked to be in his late fifties. His hair was long, curly, and never washed. He was skinny. Sickly skinny and was missing his big toe on his left foot. Matthew knew of this since Joe always wore sandals. It was something that Matthew had wanted to ask Joe about as well as the year (and make) of his black van. But once again, too muach info that Matthew didn't want to know. And then there was the issue of Joe's teeth. He didn't have that many. And Matthew had heard that the years of excessive heroin use could cause cavaties and bad gum disease. What was left in Joe's mouth were yellow teeth with black around the gum line. Matthew figured it would maybe take a year or two before Joe would loose the remaining teeth that he had. Maybe ten in all.

Joe got in the Cruiser and the sell was made. It was getting hot outside and since Matthew had turned the A/C off, it was even hotter inside. The deal was fast. Two minutes at the mose. And Matthew was back on the interstate just as fast as he could be. Heading north towards the Palm Beach Gardens exit. From there he would drive east, then north on Route one, and then back to Juno Beach.

One thing that Kimberly had never known was that under the drivers seat of Matthews PT Cruiser was a rig. (Syringe for those who may have missed it). It was given to him by Joe after he somehow got away with stealing a few after a brief stay at the hospital. This had happened a month earlier. The rig was clean and packaged tight. Waiting to be used. But not for the use of injecting heroin into someone's vein and helping to kill that person ever so slowly. No, this needle was made for the use of saving lives.

And yet, as Matthew held it in his hand, he thought to himself, *Who's to say that* banging *dope isn't saving a life?*

Sitting in the car, he realied that even though he had his rig, he didn't have a lighter, spoon, or even water to mix the the dark powder tucked away in his wallet. So he had to resort to sniffing the *stuff.* He hated to do it. Especially after spending so much time *running* it into his arms. But he wanted to celebrate. And he wanted to get high. And he wanted to be alone at the beach. And so he made a line on his bank card and used a straw from which he had lying on the car floor. It came from a large drink he had bought for Kimberly at a sub shop. He couldn't remember why the straw was saved, of even why it had been left on the car floor for so long, but it *was* there, and it *would* be used one more time.

He took a razor blade that he kept in the glove box and cut the straw at an angle. He took a look around the lot to see if anyone was there. Once he knew he was safe, he snorted a bag of the dark powder with one quick *sniff.*

It came on slow but good. And strong. Oh God, was it strong. And like I said, it was good. Oh, so good.

Matthew sat at the beach under the hot sun high and fading out. Once again he was at peace with himself anf with the universe. He listened to the waves come in and watched as hundreds of beautiful women walked by wearing bikinis and sipping on their mixed drinks. And as beautiful as they all were, not a single one could compare to the beauty that Sarah Blackwell had. There was something about her. It was damn near spiritual. And just thinking about her on the sandy beach made him feel more euphoric. He felt love for her. He knew it and wanted it to happen. And he felt happy. And he felt.... . sick.

Right there, on the beach, and just as noon time approaches, Matthew Scott was about to vomit. Heroin is a bitch of a drug. (Just a little saying that will be repeated later on). But it is being said now. And an opiate addiction is one of the most painful experience that one can ever go through. (That is if you are one of the few who can get through it alive).

He didn't do it on the beach. He did it in his car. Matthew practically ran to his PT Cruiser. He got in, leaned over into the passenger floor, and let go. It hurt him. And it made him angry with himself. *How can I be so weak?* But the answer was not that he was weak, it was that the train *ticket* that he had taken was just a tad bit stronger than his usual score. And he had never had brown heroin before. But he had heard all about it. And how good it was. Well, now he knew. Right?

He had a few towels in the back of the Cruiser. And with them, he covered the mess on the car floor with two of them and rolled down the windows. After sitting a while, Matthew started feeling better. He still had a good high going, which had helped in a way.

He took a drive up to the town of Jupiter. Once there, he stopped at one of the local car-wash stops and cleaned his car to a terrible perfection. After he was doen, he took another drive. Things were getting better. He felt so good and so thirsty. He knew better than to mix alcohol with an opiate high, but by now his train ride had subsided a bit, and so he went and stopped at a bar and had a beer.

There were one too many women sitting and drinking around him. Ost of them were with their boyfriends (or girlfriends), and looking at them all made Matthew think more of Sarah. Every girl that he saw reminded him of her. He wanted her and he wanted to see her. He *had* to see her. And he would. *Just as soon as the jackass on the payphone hangs up and goes the hell away,* he thought as he looked upon a man as he stood drunkenly with the phone in one hand and a beer mug in the other. And as aggrevating as it was for Matthew to wait, at least he had that beer to keep him occupied.

Sarah was at home when he called her. She had been drinking too and thinking about Matthew as he had been thinking about her. She told him to finish up and to come see her. Matthew hung the payphone up, went back to pay his tab, and left a three dollar tip.

Sarah and her roomates lived in a small house in a neighborhood just off of Jupiters main road, Indiantown Road, just in case you were wondering. It is a long stretch from east to west. So it made Sarah's house easy to find. The house sat at the end of a dead end street. It was one story and an ugly bright blue. But it did have one of the nicest yards around. And with the expensive cars parked out front, you would never have guessed that the people who occupied the house were poor and struggling students.

As Matthew pulled up to the house Sarah stood waiting for him. She had a bottle of cold beer and from the looks of it, it seemed to be Budweiser. Which in time would prove right. Matthew got out of the Cruiser, his eyes never leaving Sarah's. Even as he walked up the driveway to her. They never looked away from each other.

Sarah gave him a warm hug and gave him the bottle of beer that she had been drinking. It was cold in his hand. But having Sarah with him, Matthew barely noticed. They went inside and Sarah got another beer for herself. Afterwards the two went into her bedroom.

The walls to Sarah's room were a dark red. And the curtains were long and black. They ended within inches of the floor. There were the typical things that you would find in a bedroom. A dresser, desk, mirror, etc. . . And being a ladies room, lots of make-up. Only scattered everywhere. But there were two things that made Matthew curious about the room as well as Sarah herself. One was that there were no pictures on the wall. They were vacant. And rha other was that on her nightstand standing next to the bed, and right below ont of the windows, was a skull with four roses lying next to it. The skull was real. As real as the four roses that laid dying next to it. And Matthew was intrigued by what he saw. It was something that could be painted into a fine still life painting.

Sarah noticed Matthew looking at the skull (more like studying it) and came to him, standing before him and blocking his view. She put her arms around him and asked, "Are you mine, Matthew?"

"Yes, Sarah," Matthew answered while still holding onto his bottle of Budweiser beer. He put his arms around her waist. "I am yours forever. But are you mine?"

Sarah looked deeply into Matthews eyes and with a tone more serious than he could ever imagine her saying to him, she answered with one word: "Forever."

And that was when Sarah Blackwell and Matthew Scott had their first kiss. The taste of her lips was as sweet as the richest piece of chocolate. Matthew seemed to *fall* into Sarah's arms as she pulled him close to her. The feel of her breasts were sofr and full. Everything about her (and that moment) made so many things come together and the world to Matthew was once again at peace. Just like all the times sitting alone at the beach and listening to the ocean.

He loved the feel of her, and the scent of her hair as it covered her neck and back. He ran his fingers through the long dirty blonde strands. So full and long it was. And so soft was the touch of Sarah'e body as they laid on her bed and under the warmest blankets. To be inside her was pure heaven. And (besides the dope that he had banged up his arm) it was the only other heaven that Matthew knew and believed.

They loved each other for hours. Literally hours. They wouldn't leave each others side through the rest of that day and throughout the night. And that was something that they would do for each other in the times to come. They were one now. And there love for each other would be a love that would damn near kill the both of them.

One of the things that they quickly learned about each other was that they both held a love for horror films. It was nearing three in the morning, and Sarah and Mathew laid awake and looking at each other as they lay side by side in bed. They had loved each other. Over and over and over again, and still, they wanted more. But they both agreed that it would be for the best to take a break for now. And so they decided to watch something. And the only films that Sarah had to watch were horror. Mainly films by Stephen King. One of her personal faborites was the film *Silver Bullet*. And it had been too long since Matthew had seen it, and so they laid in Sarah's bed and watched the greatest film about a werewolf (that was both of their opinions) as another new morning came on.

Matthew held her close to him as she laid her head on his chest. He loved the feel and scent of her long hair. So beautiful and perfect. Matthew thought that he could die right here in her arms, that he would do it happily with not a single regret. Andas the movie was playing on Sarah's small television and in her DVD player, Matthew decided to tell her.

"Sarah,"

Sarah moved and looked at him, "Yes, Matthew."

"I love you."

There was a moment of silence and Matthew started to feel a little uneasy. He began to think that maybe he had made a mistake by telling her. But then Sarah says: "I love you too, baby. So much that I hurt when I think about it." Now she sat up and put a hand up to his face. Her dark green eyes filled with tears and she smiled. "I love you so much, Matthew."

A single tear ran down her cheek and Matthew ran a finger up, catching it. He put his finger to his lips and tasted salt as it dissolved in his tongue. "Now you won't cry anymore, I took your tears away."

They fell asleep shortly after watching the movie. They slept all day, awaking late in the afternoon.

11

Born the same year, but two months earlier than Mattew, Sarah Blackwell was raised with a younger sister by a single working mother in St. Augustine, Florida. Sarah had come down to West Palm beach to attend classes at the university. It was her second year and she still has not decided on a major as of yet. But it was alright. At least for the time being. Well, that is what her mother Joyce has been telling her.

As mentioned before, Sarah has a younger sister. Her name is Jennifer. They call her Jen for short and she is six years younger than her older sister. She recently turned fifteen. And she holds as much beauty as her older sister Sarah. Only, Jen has long brunette air and is a little more than demanding on how much attention she gets. Sarah on the other hand is more relaxed and (though she does love her baby sister) she can get easily annoyed with her. But that's not unusual.

Their father had left. He had met someone else. And that someone else happened to be someone who did not want a family. This other woman was named Lucy. A hot redhead who loved to have fun and never take any real responsibility. To Jim (the father of Sarah and Jen) it was like being young and in high school again. He left his wife and children. But he left a house and a bank account. Jen was two months and Sarah was six. The two sisters would never see their father again.

Sarah never had a lot of boyfriends since she preferred to stay a lot of her time to herself. But when she felt like it, she would have some fun. And the type of fun she would have always consisted of older boys. Boys of whom did not attend her school.

Sarah was popular. Even though she never went out of her way to be popular. And she hardly acknowledged it. Sarah is a smart girl and knew that popularity never last's. She knew it was all bullshit. Yeah she was nice and she did go to a few house parties, but all in all, Sarah Blackwell was ahead of everyone else with whom she was surrounded. And she knew it. Knew it then and knows it now.

During the summer before her senior year, she had taken a trip to the city of Jacksonville. She drover her convertible BMW (at the time was still her mothers) for she needed some time for herself. She wanted to get away from the small town life of St. Augustine. And so she headed up north. The furthest south she had gone was to Daytona, and that really didn't impress her much. But Jacksonville was better. Boring, but better.

She went to a club. She had decided this after driving around the city for an hour. It was getting late and she was anxious. She wanted to have some fun. She *needed* to have some fun. And she did.

She had never been in anything like it. And it was her first time in a club. She just couldn't drink. She was nineteen then. Cute and so innocent looking. But in a way, she was. And she once again (just like in school) stayed to herself. That was until she met Jeremy. A young, long hair, tanned, cocaine dealer. He had seen her come in and had watched to see if she was with anyone before making her move. He was good about it. He didn't come on too strong. He respected her space and bought her some drinks. All mixed. But only four of them. Sarah couldn't even finish the last. A whiskey sour. She had tried it and couldn't stand it. The first two drinks were an Island Ice Tea. The third was a Blue Hawaiian. Sarah *really* loved those. And after the first three drinks, she was feeling real good.

Sarah and Jeremy were sitting and watching people dance and drink, when he asked her if she had ever tried coke. She had told him no, and so he slid to her, a pocket mirror with four lines on it. He gave her a rolled up bill and she sniffed away without a moment of hesitation.

She loved it. It was the greatest feeling that she had ever had. Not even sex was that good. Well, not until she met Matthew.

But until then, she would see Jeremy. Just for a small time. But long enough to sleep with him a couple of times. And long enough to develop a good cocaine habit. She would see him on the weekends. They lived nearly half an hour away from each other, and so, Jeremy would call to let Sarah know when he was coming down. She had told Joyce that they were just friends. But her mother (having been young once herself) knew better. And only once did he come early. It was a Thursday. And it was near the end of their relationship. He had arrived higher than he ever had been. He wanted her and Sarah had said no. She Was watching Jenna and had promised to take her out. So instead they sat out on the front porch. She had a line while drinking a soda. Sarah spent about twenty minutes with Jeremy before she made him leave. He told her that he wold be back down that Sunday. But he never did.

Sarah's love for cocaine was one thing that she kept in secret. Not even her best friend, Becky, knew about it. After Jeremy, Sarah did find a reliable dealer. Her name was Sarah too. Only she was a Sarah with short black hair and was a little too involved within the Gothic lifestyle. She had cuts and burns on her arms. And she had (to Sarah's knowledge) a lot of boyfriends. Which was something that she herself would never do. Too dangerous and too much drama.

But none of it really mattered. As long as she had her coke when she needed it, there was never a problem.

After a week of seeing each other (which was living together), Sarah once again awoke in Matthew's arms after a long night together. He had been told by Sarah to move in with her. After their first night together, Sarah had stayed with him at the Inn. She tolerated Matthew living there for the weekend then she made him pack and move in with her. And things couldn't have been better for the two of them.

Everyone who met Matthew loved him and loved knowing that Sarah had finelly met someone who made her happy. *Really* happy.

The house was now the official placew to party. Sarah's roommates, Carmen and Anne, had new boyfriends as well. Only there relationships were not nearly as real, or strong, as Sarah's and Matthew's. They became the couple. And they would effect the lives of everyone who knre them. Some for the better. And some for the worst. Unfortunately.

Sarah and Matthew were always together. As most new couples tend to do. For they got close fast. Almost too fast. But neither one minded how fast their relationship had gone. They both absorbed each others company. It was much needed. For they were both lonely. Only they would never admit it to themselves or anyone else.

Sarah was tired of school. But then again, anyone who *does* go, gets tired after a short time of attending. As I said before, it was her second year and she still had no major yet. And her mother called every other day and would ask when her daughter would be coming home. Now that Sarah had a new boyfriend, as well as someone who she actually *wanted* to bring home, she began to think that going home was not that bad of an idea. She missed St. Augustine. She missed the long walks late at night along the waterway and the Bridge of Lions. The smell of the water. The horse carriages carrying visitors and couples along the old streets of the old city. It was her home. And she missed her best friend Becky. It had been a few months since they last talked. It was over the Christmas break. Sarah had gone home then, despite her ex's protest against it. He wanted to be with her. Chris thought that he owned her. And that was how he had treated her. And that was a great turn-off for her.

Sarah decided that it was time to go home. The only thing was that before she would take Matthew with her, they would have to get to know each other much better. She happened to be out at the moment and wouldn't see Matthew until later that night and after he came home from work.

She stopped at a gas station which just happened to stand on the corner from where Kimberly worked. After parking the car, Sarah went in to pay before filling the tank and ran right into Kimberly. Of all the times and days to run into her old friend, this day and time was not the best.

"Oh, if it isn't my dear old friend, Sarah," Kimberly says while moving up a little too close to say it. "So, what have you been up too? Seeing anybody new?"

"Yes. As a matter of fact I am," Sarah say while standing her ground. "I think you know him. His name is Matthew. Were in love and it is wonderful," Sarah says with a simle.

Sarah could see that it hurt Kimberly to hear those words. She could see it and she liked it. Just a little too much. While another thing cheered her heart, Kimberly looked awful. She looked used up and seemed to have lost one too many pounds on her already thin body. There were dark bags under her eyes and track marks running up her right hand.

She's on junk, Sarah thought to herself while holding back the urge to comment. *What a stupid bitch.*

There was a moment of silence. Sarah wanted to get moving and she did by cutting the the coversation short. "I have to get going. Matthew is waiting. You take care now."

"Oh, we *will* see each other again, so you take care of yourself," Kimberly warned. Sarah only laughed as she went to the cashier. Kimberly left and walked to work. But along that way she made sure to walk by Sarah's BMW and look back and into the station. Sarah was staring back with a look that dared Kimberly to do something. Whatever it may be, do it. Because it would come back ten times the pain. But Kimberly just kept on walking. And she did run her fingers along the side of the car.

Inside Sarah paid, fueled up, and made damn sure that she watched Kimberly and see just exactly where she walked to. For Kimberly would be seeing Sarah again. Only, sooner than she thought.

12

It happened that night. Sarah had ordered a pizza and made the order a pick-up. Matthew was left sitting on the bed. He wanted to go with her, but she insisted that he stay. She had told him that she had a surprise for him. And now it was quarter past eleven and Sarah is sitting in her car and waiting.

It said 11:28 when Sarah looked at the digital clock in her car. It always took Kimberly an half an hour to close, and at eleven thirty she walked out of the restaurant and around the back. As she did this, Sarah got out of her car and walked after her. But quietly. She did not want to make a sound. And she didn't.

Kimberly stopped at the back of the restaurant and lit up a cigarette. Sarah stood behind her and watched for a moment. She was wearing black jeans and a black t-shirt with boots to match. Her long dirty blonde hair was up in a bun. But before she made her move, Sarah looked *again* to see if there were any cameras. She had checked earlier when she had pulled into the parking lot next to the restaurant. And just as before, there were none.

She started to become angry while she watched Kimberly. She reached into her pocket and pulled out a box cutter. She pushed the blade out, then made her move.

The cold sharp steel pointed into Kimberly's neck, it hurt her and she stood as stiff as she could. She had dropped her cigarette as soon as she felt Sarah's arm come around her from behind. With one hand holding the blade and the other clenching Kimberly's shirt, Sarah spoke slowly and ever so clearly into Kimberly's ear.

"Now, you listen to me bitch, he is mine, and I am his, and you have no place in any of this. And I swear. I GODDAMN SWEAR! If you ever threaen me or my man, I will KILL YOU! I will cut your throat and watch you DIE! Understand?"

Kimberly said yes. She understood alright. She was trembling and had started to cry. Sarah couldn't stand to hear anymore of it. She lowered the blade and put it back in her pocket. She then gave Kimberly a good hard push. Kimberly fell to her knees and Sarah yelled at her to run.

"RUN YOU MISERABLE BITCH! RUN OR I WILL KILL YOU!"

And she did. Oh, did she ever. And afterwards, Sarah got back in her car, picked the pizza (just in time for the Italian restaurant to close themselves) and went home to be with her man. And that was the last that he would ever see (or hear) of her old friend Kimberly Salt.

Good riddance bitch.

13

It was when Sarah gave Matthew a line of the cocaine that she had stashed within the skull on her nightstand that Matthew quite drinking. Because once he had tried the heavenly drug (that was what they would call it) he didn't bother wasting anymore time with alcohol. And besides, he hated hangovers. But then again, I think *everybody* does.

Line after line, Sarah and Matthew got high together. Sarah had worried about telling him about the stuff. She was worried that it would upset him. She had kept her secret hidden for many years now. And it took a lot for her to reveal this part of herself to him.

"I have something to show you, Matthew," she told him as she came and sat on the bed next to him.

"Alright," he said and sat up. He had bought a new pair of bed sheets. They were hot pink. And he had bought a new comforter, blood red, to match the walls of the room.

Sarah reached over and picked up the skull. She held it in her hands for a few moments, almost forgetting about the whole thing. But she wanted so desperately to tell him. To reveal and *be* revealed. It excited her as well as Matthew. Just the thought that Sarah had something to show him, and that it involved the dirty skull, made his heart beat ten times faster.

She placed the skull between the two of them. "I want us to really get to know each other," Sarah tells him. "I want to know everything about you, and I want you to know about me." Matthew sat and listened. "And one of the tings that you need to know about me, Matthew, is that I have an addiction."

Matthew looked intrigued and Sarah reached in the skull and brought out a small bag. Within in the small bag was what they would call the heavenly drug. Looking at it made Matthew's heart beat faster. He sweated with excitement. He had never had cocaine and hoped to all the gods that that was what Sarah held in her hand.

"Well, in case you didn't figure it out already, I am holding a bag of cocaine. Its my little secret. And I have kept it for a few years now. And you afre the first to know about it." Sarah looked into Matthew's eyes. She held his hand and in a tone that was both serious and joking, she said: "I.m a coke head."

She then laughed at what she said. She set the skull back and pulled a mirror from inside a drawer from the desk. Sitting back on the bed, Sarah made four lines with a razor which Matthew failed to see her get. Sarah also pulled out a green straw (another thing that he failed to catch) and tapped it lightly on the mirror. The straw had come from a soda that she had bought at the same Wendy's (and on the same day) that they had met at. And sometimes, when Sarah is alone and cutting lines for herself, she sits back and looks at the straw and will think about that day that seemed so long ago to her. She would think about that day and Matthew and how she wished he could be with her at those moments. And now, and at this very moment, she no longer has to think or dream upon it. For she and her man have the entire night to indulge of the heavenly drug as they wanted.

And they did. Goddamn!

"I really like this stuff, Sarah."

"Well, I hope you do. I want my man to feel good."

They both took their second line and laid back on the bed. Matthew ran his fingers through her hair while Sarah rubbed his leg. The television was on but nothing good was playing. Matthew wanted to tell her about *his* stash. He wanted her to know that he had something for *her*. But not tonight. *Tommorow? Yes. I will tell her tomorrow. Better to just relax and enjoy the high that you have and stay cool.* And Matthew did. He stayed cool. And he stayed high all night with his girl in his arms.

Sarah and Matthews coke binge lasted for two days. Matthew wanted desperately to tell her about the heroin he had. But she was having too much fun. She felt relieved and free. They wrestled each other. They ate junk food. They watched horror movies. And they loved each other. Oh yes, there was a lot of *loving* in the bedroom those two days. Carmen knocked (BANGED) on the bedroom door and told them that they needed to get out of the room as well as the entire house.

Sarah had missed two days of school, while Matthew missed two days of work. He was sure he had been fired. But to his surprise (as well as Sarah's and Carmens), he was not.

It would take an entire morning for the tow of them to tire enough and sleep off the heavenly drug. And upon finding sleep, it would be night fall when the two of them would finally emerge into the night. But to the both of them, it was worth it. And Sarah never went back to class. School no longer concerned her. Matthew did. Their relationship did. And getting out of West Palm Beach and into St. Augustine did. That was all she needed to think about. Not notes, lectures, or when the next exam would be. She was done with all that. All Sarah wanted was Matthew. She, in fact, *needed* him. And she knew he needed her.

14

So high.
So unbelievably high.

Its been two weeks since his first line of cocaine. And now that first line seemed to have never happened. He doesn't remember how it felt or how big the line was. All he *does* know is that he is high. On this night he has had four lines. And he is feeling good as well as hungry. He always gets hungry on speed. But I guess that is to be expected.

Sarah was in the living room was Carmen. Her very beautiful African American roommate with whom had recently broke off an eleven month relaionship and was now feeling rather depressed. It was a bitter break up. And Carmen needed her friend to be there. She had thought she was in love. She had even wanted to be in love. But her ex had led her on. And as Sarah and Carmen sat on the couch and talked, Matthew laid on the bed high and hungry. He wantd to do so much at that moment. For he had a million emotions running through him. And what was it that he really wanted.

No. I have to put that aside. I am done with it.

No your not. You still have it. And you still know where you stashed it.

Those little eggs, well hidden in the closet and waiting to be opened. That *other* heavenly drug. A name that he has tried so hard to forget.

Heroin.

No. I have stopped.

No you haven't.

I...

want (need)

heroin.

But you can't now. For that would be bad. Very *bad. You should never mix those two highs. What, do you want to dit?*

NO!

Matthew couldn't stand the thought of it. It made him hurt. It made him itch again. And it made him start loosing his coke buzz. And that was bad. Very bad.

So he took another line. What else was there to do? Sarah was with Carmen. He was too high on speed to down it. So he took another to numb the want away.

"Sarah!" he calls out and within a moments time she is there by his side.

"What is it baby?" she asked as she sat on the bed.

"Lay with me a minute."

She did. Resting her head on his chest as he wrapped his arms around her. "What is it that you wanted? You gave me quite a scare when you yelled out like that." She listened to his heart beat. It always relaxed her. It made her smile.

"I just wanted to be with you my darling."

There was one more line left and it was for Sarah. It was a real good one. Three in one. She ran it through the straw in one deep sniff. Afterwards, she gave her man a passionate kiss before going back out into the living room to comfort Carmen. Matthew laid on the bed and felt blood run out of his nostril.

Later, after Carmen went to her room, Sarah and Matthew spent another night within each others arms. It was a good way to end the evening. Especially after Sarah had to hear about how Carmens ex had used her and lied to her about a million and one things. Even while Sarah sat and listened to her friend she was eager to leave her and spend time with her man. It had been a long day. And now it had become an even longer night. All she wanted while she sat and listened was for the night to end.

Matthew was deep inside her. He loved her and told her so. "I love you too," she said back to him as she looked into his eyes. He became lost in hers and they held each other close.

So warm, he thought. *My God, she is so warm.*

15

Catching a cold was one thing that Matthew had never thought possible from taking cocaine.But it *does* happen, and he *did* get sick. It happened one night after he had taken eight lines in less than two hours. He was alone and had nothing to do. That same night, he had gone to meet Sarah at a club. She wanted him to dance with her but he was so high that he could only stand against the wall by the dance floor and watch her and Carmen dance with each other. He was so numb. And he wouldn't have a drink. He was done with all that. And ever since that night, he has had a cold.

"It lowers your immune system," Sarah told him as he laid with her in bed and trying not to sneeze. Again.

"I wish I had known that. If I had, then I would have never taken so much."

Sarah gave him a kiss and pulled the blankets over him tight. She was taking care of him, and she loved it. "My poor sick boy," she would say to him. "I am here for you."

Time seemed to move fast for the both of them. And the more time that moved ahead, the more time was pushed back for their move to St. Augustine. And they needed to move. They needed to get away from the city of West Palm Beach.

And they would.

But not until Sarah would be introduced to that *other* heavenly drug. Soon it would happen. Soon they would begin. Soon, Sarah and Matthew would journey into what *they* call Hell. Soon.

16

The best thing that would ever happen for this total piece of trash was Sarah Blackwell. But Chris, being the typical male with "you're my girl and I own you," type of attitude, took her for granted. He is too much of a backwoods redneck to know a good thing when it sits in front of him. He drinks too much. He takes too many drugs. And he is about to make a big mistake by trying to screw with matthew Scott.

He had been known to be quite a bully. Only, the people that he *can* bully are kids. He looks, and sure as hell acts, like a tough guy. But put face to face with someone with whom he has pissed off, and he runs like the coward he is. Nothing more than a boy trapped within a grown mans body.

"STUPID LITTLE BITCH!" Sarah had yelled at him the day that she had left him.

Chris had to move out of the apartment that he had been living in with two other guys. Two guys who happened to attend the same college that Sarah once had. They were both friends of Sarah. But of course. For how else would that ungrateful redneck live in an apartment off the beach?

And as soon as Sarah had let her two friends know that she had dropped him, they had kicked him out. Now Chris lives with his mother. He has no job and only one friend. A boy named Joey. He lives within a nearby trailer park and owns just as many felonies as does Chris. Mainly since the two of them commit these crimes together as well as get busted together.

On the day that Chris had decided to talk to Sarah about the break-up, he had heard about a warrant set out for her arrest. She had failed to appear in court for due to a possessions charge two months earlier. He figured that this was a good day as any to call her. He would use *that* as his axcuse for the call. Then he would turn the conversation towards the two of them. It would work. It had to work. He *needed* it to work. He had only had sex with one girl since the break-up. And that was because he could afford it.

He felt good. He had taken a shower, shaved all the hair off his head and face, and smoked a joint. Yes, Chris was walking tall today. Nothing in the world to do except bother other people.

He stopped at a corner market from his mothers house. He used the payphone next to the building. He stood there under the hot Florida sun waiting for her to pick up. As he stood there a Palm Beach police car pulled and parked by him. Two cops sat and watched him. They were both big men. And they sat in the car during the entire conversation and watched.

17

"Hi, Chris. What do you want?" Sarah asked with zero interest. "I really don't have time for you right now. Or *ever*, for that matter."

"I just want to tell you that I miss you and that I think that I derserve another chance." Chris had actually forgotten all about telling her about the warrant. Once again it was about him. Just like when they wee together. He let his emotions do the talking for him.

"Chris, I left you for a reason. You are just no good for me. And besides, I needed a real man. And just to let you know... I got one."

"But I..."

Click.

Chris walked away from the payphone with a mix of emotions. He wanted to do many things. He wanted to fight. Take more drugs. Cry. But all that he would do is spend time in jail. The two cops who had parked and watched him had also followed him home. They waited for him to make that one mistake that they had waited for.

Chris took out of his pocket another joint and lit it up. He was arrested too fast to think about. He would spend the next three months sitting in a cell and crying for his release. And upon that release he would make yet another mistake. He would receive the beating of a lifetime.

18

It was early that Sunday morning when the police showed at the house. Two cars and two officers. They both walked together to the front door. One of the officers complained that it was too cold for him. It was now nearing seven thirty that morning. And maybe it was a little too cold. It had rained the night before. And hurricane season was just around the corner.

It was Carmen who had answered. She was wearing her nightgown. It was soft pink. And as she stood next to the opened door, she couldn't help but feel the hang-over coming on strong as the two officers waited for her to speak. "Yes?" she asked irritably.

"Does a Sarah Blackwell live here, and if so, is she home?" The asking officer placed both hands on his belt and looked at her. Both of them did. All of her. And they made no effort to hide it. They stood quietly and waited for Carmens response.

"She's in that room," Carmen pointed as the two officers walked in. As the second one passed, he looked down at Carmen's legs and gave her a smile. Carmen felt rage run through her and ran to her room. She slammed the door, hard.

"Sarah Blackwell, this is the Palm Beach Police, here to serve you with a warrant for your arrest. Pleaase open the door."

Sarah was already awake. She had awoken upon Carmen slamming her bedroom door. Matthew never stirred. They had both had another long night, and had only slept for three hours by the time the two officers had knocked at her door.

She knew immediately what was happening. A first she sat in bed and didn't move. Her heart was pounding fast and her head was spinning. She was clothed by one of Matthews Iron Maiden t-shirts. Matthew was clothed with a pair of shorts that he wore to bed. An half empty bottle of vodka sat next to the skull with roses. Matthew had wanted to drink, but he had gone so long without any alcohol, that it would be stupid for him to pick up the habit again. For Sarah, drinking was never a problem. She would dance and laugh and love. And Matthew enjoyed watching her. He loved to watch her jump and spin around the bedroom. Her long hair flowing around her neck. Seeing her smile as she looked at him drunk and happy. Looking at her as she stood there, only hours ago, in her black bra and panties.

But there was nothing that he would enjoy about this morning. There were three hard bangs on their bedroom door as one of the officers began to loose their patience. Matthew awoke to see Sarah getting dressed. He asked her what was going on and she had said not to worry and then told the officers to hold on a minute longer.

"We have a warrant for your arrest, Miss Blackwell."

"Sarah, what the hell is he talking about?"

Sarah went to him. She had thought about jumping out the window and making a run for it. It was a brief thought. But what she really wanted to do was hold Matthew. He looked so tired and all she wanted to don was hold him and let him fall asleep in her arms.

"Matthew, I should have told you, but I forgot. I honestly forgot," she told him as she tried to hold back her tears.

"Forgot what?"

The door opened and the two officers came in. Sarah turned and looked at them while she tried to hide Matthew from them.

"Sarah Blackwell," an officer said, "I am here to take you into custody for this warrant. I need you to turn and place your hands behind your back." Sarah did as was told and was read her rights. She looked at Mattehw as she was handcuffed. She wanted to cry. She was embarrassed and couldn't tell what the expression on Matthew's face meant to tell her.

"Sarah, what is all of this?" he asked her quietly. He did not want the officers to hear them speak.

"I should have told you, but I forgot. I am so sorry, baby."

"Don't worry. I'll get you out as soon as I can," Matthew assured her.

And then she was gone. Taken away from him and their home. Taken and placed in a cell with three other women with whom had been arrested the night before.

As Sarah sat in the back of that police car, and as she sat at the magistrates desk, and as she sat at another desk at the jail while an officer asked her weight, height, eye color, and if she had taken any drugs within the last twenty four hours, all she could think about was Matthew.

Her hands trembled as she was asked these questions. And she tried her best to stat calm and answer each question completely and honestly. She knew that she could be put away for awhile when she goes to court. In two months. But she would not cry. She wanted too. Especially after hearing the amount of her bail. Which she doesn't have. Or even Matthew.

Or does he? Money is something that has never been discussed. And he always *has money to spend when needed. But then again why would we ever need to talk about money. Our relationship* isn't *based on money. It is* based on love. Real love. Sarah thought these things while sitting in her cell. She had tried to call home but no one answered. And to keep herself calm, she told herself that the reason why no one had answered was because Matthew and Carmen were out trying to get money for her bail.

And they did.

Three days later.

19

When she was bailed out that Wednesday, Matthew had banged a twenty bag of heroin. He couldn't resist the urge anymore. It was too strong for him. As anyone who *has* taken the drug would know. And he still didn't know as to exactly why Sarah was arrested. Carmen wouldn't tell him. And he couldn't call her mother. She was not, under any circumstances, to know about this.

Matthew wouldn't get out of the car. He was paranoid about himself being arrested for how high he was. So he waited. The jail released the inmates after eight thirty every morning. He had discovered this fact after posting Sarah's bail Tuesday evening. It didn't make much since to him. And it may have been the only reason why he had faded after getting back to the house. He had been more than mad. He was damn near loosing his cool.

They didn't speak much on the drive back to the house. Sarah was angry, and yet, curious as to why she couldn't get a hold of Matthew (or Carmen) four the past three days. She would look at Matthew, and he at her, but they wouldn't speak. They both didn't know how to handle the situation that they found themselves in.

The drive home couldn't have ended fast enough. Even as high as Matthew was, time moved too slow for him.

It was silent in the house, and even more silent in the bedroom. Sarah had walked in first and waited for Matthew to shut the door to say her first word to him.

"Why couldn't I get a hold of you, Matthew?"

"I was busy trying to raise the money to get you out," Matthew told her as he took off his shoes. He didn't want a fight. But he knew Sarah was more than upset and made sure to watch what he said.

"YOU COULDN'T HAVE ANSWERED THE PHONE WHILE YOU WERE AT IT!" Sarah screamed. Her hande were shaking again and she was seeing red. "The whole time I was locked up all I thought about was you. It drove me crazy. Not seeing you. Not being able to touch you," she was beginning to cry, "I wanted to kill myself. I had to stay in that place away from you with these other degenerates, and the one person who I care about more than my own life doesn't even answer the damn phone to know that I'm okay, and that she misses and LOVES HIM!"

What really made the situation worse was that Matthew was high on junk and it was making him distant from her. And Sarah *knew* that there was something. She *didn't* know what it was, and it was hurting her more. Much more than she already felt.

"Okay, Sarah," Matthew said as he stood close to her. "I have to tell you something. And it involves how I, and Carmen, got the money to get you out."

Hearing Matthew say those words to her made Sarah feel intrigued and no longer upset. And she couldn't help but notice how Matthew continually scratched at his arm. And so she sat on the bed and asked Matthew to do the same.

There was a few seconds of silence as they sat next to each other. It seemed to take forever for Matthew to find the words to tell her. But he finally did.

"Sarah, Carmen and I had to sell some things to raise the money we needed to get you."

"What things?"

"Drugs."

"What drugs? If you tell me you sold *our* supply, I will seriously hurt you. As much as I love you, I will."

Matthew figured that either way Sarah would want to hurt him regardless of *what* he sold. The situation to him seemed to be a double edged blade. He's screwed either way.

"Train. I mean heroin. Carmen and I sold some heroin," he told her as he looked doen at the floor. He itched all over. Especially at the tip of his nose.

Sarah looked at Matthew with a look that scared him. He was sure it was disgust. But it could have been shock. But either way, it made him cringe. He felt chills run over him. And he finally gave in and scratched at his arms and nose.

There was that silence again. It seemed to last forever. He looked back down at the floor. He could still feel Sarah's eyes upon him. Still upon him.

"I love you, Matthew," she finally said. She placed a hand on the back of his neck and began to message him gently.

"I love you too, Sarah," Matthew replied. He felt a nod, but fought it off.

"Your into dope then?"

"Yes."

"Nothing will change the way I feel for you. You are mine and I am yours. I only wish that you had told me earlier. You remember our agreement? No secrets?"

"I remember," Matthew says and looks at her. "I was going to tell you a few weeks ago, but you were having too much fun with that coke and I didn't want to spoil your mood. Guess you can say I'm a junkie."

Sarah slapped him. Hard.

"YOU ARE NOT A JUNKIE!" Sarah screamed into his ear. "You are Matthew Scott. You are my man, and one day you and I will spend the rest of our lives as husband and wife."

Matthew couldn't tell at the moment which was worse. Getting the taste slapped out of his mouth. Or the fact that he was loosing his high. He figures it to be 50/50. But regardless, he sat and took his *medicine*. A medicine named Sarah Blackwell.

"Junkies are losers. And I for one do *not* associate with losers."

"I am sorry, Sarah. But I did what I had to do to get you out. And..."

"Did you take any?"

"Yes," Matthew answers ashamedly. "Carmen and I had some last night. And I banged a bag this morning."

"Well, no wonder you wouldn't get out of the car," Sarah says and laughs. It was strained, but it was a laugh no less.

"You want to try some?" Matthew asked bravely. Sarah was not herself this morning. But under the circumstances, who could blame her?

"Yes. And no. The thought of that stuff scares me."

"I know what you mean. I was scared too. At first. My first time trying it, I snorted it. And to my surprise, it was good. *Very* good."

Yes, the climate in the room was changing. And for the better.

"Well, I haven't gotten high in four days. And I want to. So cut me a line and lets get on with it."

Matthew knew all to well when she mentioned getting on with it. And what *it* could do.And so while Sarah took her shower and changed her clothes, Matthew made two lines with from the supply that he had left for him. Only this time it would be better. This time he would not have to feel guilty about it. He would share this time (and others) with Sarah. And it was all happening so fast. And it would go even faster after they... .

20

Sarah felt the burn immediately. Snorting heroin is not the best way to take it. But it *is* a lot safer. If taking heroin is ever safe? But she loved it. And Matthew loved her even more for loving it too.

They both laid on the bed and listened to the radio while staring at the ceiling. They both itched like crazy. But it was good. Oh, so good.

"I love it, baby," Sarah said to him as she scratched her nose. She laid her head on his chest. It felt so good to her to feel him and hear his heart. She wanted more. And just like Matthew, she was instantly addicted to the high. "Give me more. I want more. MORE!"

"Okay. Let me get up and cook some up."

"Wait. What do you mean by *cook* some up?"

They were both sitting up now. Sarah looked scared. And knowing that, Matthew put his arm around her and settled her nerves.

"Its called *banging*. It won't hurt. And the high is ten times better. Way better then snorting or smoking. And it won't take long to cook. And I will be very careful with you. Okay?"

Sarah relaxed a little. Then put the fate of her *life* in Matthews hands by saying: "Okay, baby. I trust you."

She sat on the edge of the bed and watched as Matthew pulled out his syringe, lighter, and dope. She watched as he cooked up the drug, and was sweating over it. It even turned her on. While watching him, she ran her hands over her legs and thought about all the times that she had Matthew inside her. She could feel the heat building within her. She laid back and waited for Matthew to be done.

Matthew sat next to her as she laid on the bed. Mattehw told her to keep her arm straight while he tied a tie around her arm. They both watched her vein appear. Thick and dark purple it pulsed. The sexual feelings that she had before wee *now* heightened.

"Just relax. I'll try not to hurt you," Matthew tells her as her gets ready.

"I love you, baby," Sarah tells him as she waits.

"I love you too," he replies.

The syringe went in nice and smooth, with little pain. Matthew couldn't help but notice the warmth of the needle as he held it within his hand. It was in and out within seconds. As was Sarah.

He cooked up his fix and banged it. He laid down next to Sarah and they faded in and out together while listening to the radio.

Sarah had never felt the way she did now. It was the complete opposite of speed. But that is to be expected.

She loved cocaine. Had loved it since the first taste those few years back. But this high was *so* much more than she could ever imagine. With speed she was happy. And now, with heroin, she was at peace. Nothing mattered. Not even Matthew mattered to her. Which was saying a lot. For she loved him dearly. Loved him to a sick distraction. But noe even her feelings for hinm could withhold the effects of this new drug known to her as *train*.

"I am in heaven, Matthew. We are in heaven together." She laid her head on his chest again. "I feel so good. Don't you, baby?"

"Iv'e always thought that this is what death was like. Werer dead in heaven, my love."

Sarah laughed at what Matthew had said. It wasn't that it was all that funny. It was just a reaction to the high. She really *did* feel as good as she thought she did. No mind tricks played here. They laid together for nearly an hour, lost within their heaven. They loved each other afterwards. It was one of the best they had ever had. Very intense and *painful*. While inside her, and caught within the moment, Matthew bit Sarah above her shoulder. She had winced a little, but told him to keep on going. To bite her harder, while she bit on his chest. Bit so hard that she nearly drew blood. They were still discovering each other. And it was equally exciting as well as painful.

21

There descent into hell wasn't fast (unlike others), theirs was slow. Slow and painful.

It had been a week since they had banged up. They had to be careful since Sarah's release from jail required her to see a parole officer every Friday. And take a drug test whenever it was convenient for *them*. And because of this fact, Sarah and Matthew would only ride the train on the weekends. It was safer that way (at least that's what they thought). But when the law is on your back, there is never a good time to screw around. And heroin doesn't stay in ones system for long. And because of this fact, their new *habit* progressed faster thanit should.

As the weeks passed, the supply between cocaine lessened, as the supply of heroin grew. Slowly, Sarah's first love died out as her new love moved in. And little by little, Sarah's and Matthew's appearance became more evident of their addiction. They both lost weight. And the light tan skin that they both had worn, slipped away to a dead pale white. They wouldn't leave the house unless the sun was down. (Or if Sarah had to go for one of her drug screenings). They continued to bite each other and had become involved with methods of bondage while in the bedroom. They both looked as though they had not slept in days on end. (Even though they slept quite a bit). And to top it all off, they were irritable with other people. They shut out their friends and family as much as they possibly could.

It was a good two months into their addiction that Sarah's arm became infected after the needly missed her vein. Her arm, from the pit to her shoulder, was swollen with blood and puss. And it was three days from the night that it had happened that she finally decided to go see a doctor.

She never gave a straight answer to the questions asked by the doctors on how it had happened. But they had already known. And they had no problem letting Sarah know just how they felt about the whole matter.

The doctors and nurses were more than rude to her. And they didn't really say all that much with their *own* mouths. She was told plenty by them when she was given a pamphlet on opiate addiction right before leaving.

Her arm had been cut open with a scapel after receiving a shot to numb the pain. The operation took a good fifteen minutes, and left a scar that would never fade.

That night Sarah had a dream. She dreamt that she was lying on the beach. The same beach that she and Matthew had met at that long time ago. It was nearing two that afternoon, and she was stretched out on a towel while wearing a red bikini. The weather was warm, and the breeze warmer. She had the radio and and an open beer next to it. And there were others on the beach as well. Family's and couples. Random people walking by. Some of them walking their dog.

It was a perfect day. Too perfect. And even as she dreamed it, she could even *feel* it.

She closed her eyes after a long sip of her beer. She pulled her sunglasses over her eyes and rested her hands on her smooth tan stomach. And there wa a moments silence right before the terror started.

First she heard the screams, and she pulled her sunglasses off. Sitting up she looked upon a dark figure who walked out onto the hot sand from the ocean water. The dark figure was a man. She could see it. And she could see that he was pale. Pale white and dead. Looking at the dark man made her stomach turn. He walked slowly towards her, and as he did, her arms began to shake and itch. She scratched at them. And as she did, the skin peeled away while blood flowed over her fingers and hands. She started to cry. And she wanted to stop scratching but couldn't. And the more she tried, the faster the dark figured man came to her. And the closer he came, the more she itched. So bad that she began to scratch all over while peeling away more skin. Until finally, the dark figured man was standing over top her and looking down into her scared eyes.

It was Mathew.

Sarah cried out to him and held out her bloody hands. But he only looked down upon her and laughed and spat at her. She continued to cry. Only harder now. And as she did, she covered her face with her bloody hands.

"I have something for you," he said to her.

"Go away, Mattehw. Please... Go... AWAY!"

"I have something for you," Matthew tells her again. And as dreams will do, Sarah was no longer on the hot sand crying. Now she was being pulled into the salty water while screaming and digging her bloody fingers into the wet sand. Shells, broken and whole, ran under her fingernails.

"I have something for you," is all that Sarah heard as the salty waves came crashing over her body, face, and eyes. She screamed out one last time before she...

Awoke early the next morning and looked at Matthew as he slept next to her. Her first instinct was to kick him. But it was just a dream. And she knew it wouldn't be fair to take anything out on him. So instead, Sarah laid in the bed and stared at the ceiling and thought about everything and nothing at all.

She tried to sleep. But it was of no use. And she really needed to. She was very tired, and after the long week that she had had and living with an infected arm, sleep was the best thing for her. Not drugs. Not even sex. Just sleep. And now she couldn't even do that. And since she couldn't sleep herself, she figured that Matthew shouldn't either. And so, with one hard slap to the side of his head, Matthew was awoken from his own deep sleep.

"Sometimes, I want to cut your throat and kiss your tears," she said to him after he had awoken with a startled look upon his tired face.

"And how are you this morning, my dear?"

"Don't get smart with me," Sarah said to him sharply, and yet, jokingly at the same time.

There was a moment of silence as the two of them looked at each other. And without sating a single word to the other, Sarah and Matthew thought about how much fun it would be to beat the other until blood flowed.

Their moment of silence ended when they hugged and held each other tightly. It was still too early for them to take that extra step.

Matthew had stopped working at the reastaurant and had picked up selling drugs as his new form of employment. He sold a little of everything just to see what sold the best. And to no surprise, marijuana, cocaine, and heroin, sold *very* well. Matthew had never cared for marijuana. It always made him tired and uninspired. But it *did* kame him a lot of money. And that was just fine with the two of them.

The nice thing about selling drugs was that it was sold to the same people every time. Which was a lot of stress off his mind. Matthew did not want to get busted. The very thought of being locked away scared him. And because of that fear, he was very careful not to draw a lot of attention to himself.

Sarah sold as well. Only, she didn't give a damn who she made money off of. She was vicious. And she would not take no from anyone. If she had to, she would threaten and intimidate as much as she could to get that one sell. And between the two of them, they had made eight thousand by the end of the first month. By the second, they had to stop. Sarah's court date was coming up, and she had wanted to stay clean and out of trouble untio she got through that big day.

Sarah's run in with the law happened one night while riding with Chris and Joey to Broward County. The three of them were in a car that happened to have a taillight out. And that had been the reason why the arresting officer had pulled the car over.

She had not smoked any of the marijuana that Chris had brought along for the ride. But Joey was more than happy to take that little extra that was offered to him. And when the officer had pulled them over, there was still a thick cloud of smoke that had settled throughout the vehicle, even though they had all the windows down.

All three were arrested. The officer had forgotten all about the broken tail light as soon as he had approached the drivers side window. He could smell the aroma of the drug, as well as see the smoke running out the windows. The car belonged to Chris's mother. An eight-five Ford Crown Victoria. Bought it brand new and right off the lot, just to have her sone arrested in it years later.

At first they were told to hold their hands up and keep them up at all times. Two other cars showed up and they were then told to get out. They were searched for any drugs and weapons. Sarah had her wallet and some cash.

Chris and Joey both were holding a knife. And Chris was the only one holding. The three were handcuffed and taken in. Three cars for three people. It was a rather odd thing to do, but who were they to ask questions.

They were all charged with possesion. (Even though Sarah was not found with holding anything). But she was in the car. And that was enough for the arresting officer.

Sarah was released from jail first. She was in only two days. Where as Chris and Joey were in two weeks. They had *other* charges still on their records, and while sitting on the side of Interstate 95, those charges were brought about. Sarah had no idea what the two boys were in trouble for. And she could care less. Even till this day.

Sarah had a cousin who lived close by, and it was him who had bailed her out the first time. And it was just her luck. A month later he would be gone, living within the mountains of New Hampshire.

She was told to come up and visit after all this mess was resolved. And she had even been given money for a lawyer (which was never even used for that purpose), for her case. A case which was surely to be dropped.

22

High.
So very high.

Is all that Matthew could think as he sat on the couch. He had gone to buy more heroin with two friends of his. Two fifty bags. He had decided to snort his while Sarah banged hers.

"Why not, Matthew?"

"I'm just not in the mood for it."

"Come on," Sarah said as she tugged at his arm. "Let me *bang* you. Okay? Please with sugar on top?" Sarah says and smiles.

"NO!" Matthew says sharply. He was becoming irritated with her. She just wouldn't take no for an answer.

"Well fine then," Sarah tells him angrily and walks back into the bedroom and slamming the door behind her.

After Matthew had snorted his, he had wished that he had two more. It wasn't that big of a purchase. Even for a fifty. He thought again of how they needed a new dealer.

It had been a while since they had had any speed. And Matthew was starting to get a little nerve for it. They have spent a good while Dead In Heaven (as the two of them called it). Especially since that's how the twoof them have been. Fading and itching. Itching and fading. It was all so beautiful to him.

By now, Sarah was banging up herself. Matthew had stopped doning it for her weeks ago. He didn't like the decision. He wanted to continue to help her out. There was just too many things that could go wrong. And he would get nervous every time she went to do it.

"I'm willing to take us as far as we can go," Sarah told him as she laid her head in his lap. She was sweating, and her nose was already red from scratching at it too much.

"I have always felt that way about you," Matthew told her as he ran his fingers through her hair.

"I just feel so good about you, Matthew. I always have. And for a long time I tried to ignore those feelings that I have for you. And us. But it was hurting me too much to do that."

"I knew that you were holding back. And I decided not to push for anything. I figured that if it was meant to be, then it would. And so I just enjoyed every minute that I could get with you."

"I love you so very much," Sarah tells him.

"And I love you too."

Sarah gave him a long and very passionate kiss. A kiss that was more intensified by the high that they were lost within. They kissed and explored each other as they had done so many times before. Then it was to the bedroom where they didn't leave unitl the next morning.

Sarah became dope sick. And now, for the second time, her arm is swollen. But luckily for her, it is not as bad as the first time. She had saved some of the antibiotics from the first time, and used what was left to heal herself. But as far as being sick, well, she would just have to wait it out.

The syringe used was shared between the two of them. Not the best of ideas, but with them there was fear of anything. For they were in love. Sarah and Matthew had actually wanted to *be* one another. They had wanted to be a part of each others body. And to share the same blood. And they would. And it would be very painful. It was only a matter of time now.

The same day that Sarah had her court date their dealer was busted while trying to sell to an undercover cop. Sarah was found not guilty of all charges. The main thing being that she never had anything on her. She was getting a ride. And was never informed of the drugs or weapons being brought along for the long drive.

While Sarah was at the courthouse Matthew was trying to get a hold of their dealer. He had called eight times with no avail. And it was upon giving up when their dealer called him. From jail. Just to let hime know the bad news. Bail was set for five thousand. Matthew was told to stay cool. And was given the directions to a new dealers house. All of this was done very carefully, you understand.

Matthew hung-up the phone, got off the couch, and went into the bedroom. He was pacing. He was desperate. He *needed* his fix. He was shaking and sweating. His lungs hurt as well as his lower back. He was starting to get sick as well. And it had been hours since his last fix. And it was at this moment that Matthew realized just how addicted he has become.

23

Methadone. A junkies best friend when that train ride has ended. There are other pills to take. But in this case, its just going to be methadone. And yes, it would be safe to say that Sarah and Matthew are junkies. Although it is best to never mention the word when the two are around. Especially Sarah.

Because their dealer was arrested and would spend a few moths locked up, Matthew used his friends advice and found the address and dealer. But this dealer didn't just sell heroin. She sold methadone pills as well. It was somewhat of a let down for the two lovers. But it would do the job until they found someone else. At least that was how they were looking at the situation.

Matthew had wanted to go to Miami to find someone, but Sarah had protested. Matthew had argued that they had never tried the pills before, and so they might not work for them. But when he finally gave in and listened to Sarah, he (as well as herself) found that the methadone pills worked just right.

Their new supplier is Lindsey. A short brunette with a nose ring and a tattoo of a wizard on her back. She had been into the heroin scene for years. Then went to rehab where she picked up her new habit, methadone.

"I personally think these pills are better than *train*. But then again, these pills are made to be better. I think," Lindsey told Matthew upon their first meeting. He ended up with four pills. It was nearing two that afternoon when he had gotten home. Sarah was asleep in the bedroom. She had kept a secret stash of heroin, safely hidden, and forgotten about unitl today. She had found it while doing a little house cleaning.

Matthew could never keep a stash for long. He would usually take all of his purchase. And all at one time.

He was quiet as he entered the house. He knew Sarah had been feeling a little under the weather since her court date. And he also knew that a lot of it had to do with her being dope sick. And it was for that one reason that

Sarah had hid her stash. And luckily for her, she came across it ealier this day.

"Hi, baby," Matthew said as he laid next to her on the bed. He was careful not to be careless with his words. "I have something for you."

Sarah had awoken when he opened the bedroom door. Matthew told her that he was sorry for awakening her. And she in return told him that it was all cool.

"What is it that you have for me?" she asked with a soft voice and tired eyes.

"I bought some methadone pills. Four of them. These should do just as good as train. I was told that they are actually better. But I'm not sure I can believe that."

"Okay, Matthew. Just give me a few more minutes and I, I mean we, can take them together.Alright?"

"Alright."

"I love you," she told him as she closed her eyes and nodded off again. Matthew became suspicious. Even if Sarah had taken some heroin, there was nothing that he could do about it now. And why would he? She is *still* here with him. And she *still* loves him. And so Matthew laid next to her and fell asleep himself. He would awake an hour later after hearing Sarah getting herself dressed after taking a shower.

Matthew looked upon her pale, skinny body. Not too skinny. But she could use a good ten pounds to her figure.

Sarah sat on the bed. She was wearing an old pair of jeans and one of Mattews *HIM* t-shirts. "My hand is numb," she tells him. "Do you remember that one night when you banged one in my hand?"

"Yes."

"Well, right here has been numb ever since. I think you must have hit a nerve and killed it. Or something like that." Sarah was rubbing the top of her right hand and showed Matthew the spot. "That's the nature of the game, I guess."

"Sometimes," Matthew replied. He took one of the methadone pills and gave one to Sarah. They both laid on the bed and waited.

"I was told it takes bout and hour for this stuff to kick in."

"An hour," Sarah complained. "But I don't want to wait that long." Sarah kicked her legs like a child would when having a fit. Only she wasn't really having one. It was just one of those things that she would do if she wanted Matthew to entertain her. And luckily for Matthew, doing something that was entertaining to Sarah *always* consisted something sexual.

Sarah and Matthew liked it very much. Both of them lying in bed together. Sarah had her jeans off and was wearing the same *HIM* t-shirt. Matthew wore nothing.

"This stuff is good, but I would rather bang some train if given a choice," Sarah said while looking up at the ceiling.

"It is almost the same as train. But I will have to agree that I would rather run some train instead. Especially with you."

"Oh, we will when the time is right."

"I wish the time was now. I would bang two eggs if I could," Matthew says and scratches at his arm.

"Hey, your getting me worked up. I don't like it."

"Sorry."

She moved over a little more so she could feel his body against hers. She laid her head on his chest again as Matthew ran his fingers through her hair. There was a moment of sinlence as the two of them enjoyed their *altered* state together.

"What are you thinking about, Matthew?"

"I was just thinking about the beach and getting a new rig. And you."

"Well, what about me?"

"Just about how we came together and how long we have been together. I am also curious as to what will happen with us in the near future."

"Yeah, I think about that stuff too. But then it scares me and so I take more train and I no longer care anymore. I am just happy to be with you now, baby."

"I am happy too. And I never want this to end."

"It won't, Matthew," Sarah promised and gave him a kiss on his chin.

Sarah took another half pill, while matthew took the other plus one more. They had some beers and went to the beach. The sun was just setting at the time of their arrival. And the sky over them intrigued the both of them. Especially in the state of mind that they were in.

The rest of the evening was *very* relaxing. But the next morning was something different. Matthew awoke feeling sick to his stomach. And he knew immediately it was from the methadone pills. That was the one thing Lindsey had failed to mention to him. That the pills have a time release, and that it would take nearly a whole day to get the drug out of his system.

He couldn't sleep, eat, or even drink water without running into the bathroom and getting sick.

"You took too much, Matthew," Lindsey told him after he called. "You should hav just taken one and stayed at that."

"Well, I will remmeber that next time."

"How's Sarah feeling?"

"She's fine. She had one and a half pills, and a few beers."

"Just one for now on, okay?"

"Alright, Lindsey."

"I wish that I was there to make you feel better," Lindsey told Matthew before hanging-up.

Since he was sick, Matthew stayed in bed and drew pictures. All of them were images of death. Dead women and children. Rotting skin with maggotts eating their flesh. He was in no way religious, but he drew a cross surrounded by dark clouds. On this cross were eyes. And surrounding the cross were stars. Stars which pointed south. "Down towards the devil," he had told Sarah.

"Very nice and disturbing, baby." Sarah gave him a look and patted him on the head.

"out of fire and brimstone he will come," Matthew told her and smiled a rather sinister grin. Sarah made a nag sound and stuck her tongue out at him while she slapped her hand on her ass. She walked out of the bedroom and into the kitchen to fix some food. Just the thought of eating made Matthew feel sick again. But this time he hekd it in.

"I just want this to go away!" he shouted.

He placed the picture aside and turned onto his side. He held his stomach. He was thinking now that it probably would have been better if he *had* gotten sick while he had the chance.

Sarah made herself a chicken salad sandwhich with chips and a beer. A nice cold bottle of Budweiser. It was almost as good as heroin. At least she thought so. She walked back into the bedroom to find Matthew on his side and trying his best not to get sick. But at the sight of her sandwhich, he had to get up and go into the bathroom.

"Well, it could be worse, baby," Sarah said while he was hunched over the toilet seat. It was as though she really didn't care about him being sick. She just sat on the bed and ate her sandwhich and drank her beer.

"Go to hell, Sarah!" Matthew said back. It wasn't really shouted. And there was no anger in his voice. It just came out. And it took Matthew (as well as Sarah) by surprise.

"Well then, why don't you come with me then, bitch," she replied coldly. She sat and waited for a response. But nothing came. So she continued to eat her sandwhich and drink her beer. "That's what I thought," she said with a mouth full of food.

In the bathroom, Matthew was trying his best not to yell back at her. He didn't want to. He *never* wanted to. He loved her. And he always wanted things between them to stay cool. He decided to take a shower.

"Matthew, are you alright?" Sarah asked after hearing the water turn on and seeing the door shut. She had expected him to come back out and lay on the bed next to her. And when that didn't happen, she started to become concerned. She started to have images of him hurting himself.

She waited another minute, then placed the plate of food to the side and got up. But by then the shower had turned off, and she could hear the sound of the shower curtain being pulled aside.

"Matthew?"

"Yes."

"I'm sorry for earlier. Are you feeling alright? Or, at least, are you feeling better?"

"Not really. And I'm sorry too."

"That's okay. I love you."

"And I love you too."

But the truth of the matter was that they both had liked it. Without saying a word, they both liked the feeling of anger towards each other. Because you can't always love someone. Sometimed you just want to rip your loved ones head right off. And that is okay. Just as long as you don't actually do it.

It was as if a miracle had happened. A new episode of *The Simpsons* came on and Mattew got to see it. So that made his night a little better even though he was still sick.

"Have a drink with me."

"Sarah, you know I have stopped drinking. What has it been three months now?"

"I don't know, Matthew. I don't keep count over unnecessary things."

There was that attitude again. And Matthew knew that if he wasn't so sick that he would say something back. But he just kept his cool and left it alone.

"I'm sorry again, baby. Its just that I haven't had any train and it is really getting to me."

"Its alright. Just remember that I'm not the one who has cut you off."

"I know baby. I love you."

"I love you too."

"Maybe we should go back to speed. Just until we get some train. You know?"

"Sure, Matthew. We haven't had any if that for some time now. It might be good for us. But not until you are at a hundred percent. I can't stand the thought of you overdoing it and ending up in a hospital. That would kill me. So not until you are better. Okay?"

"Sure. Alright."

That night Matthew had a dream. He wasn't sure as to why he had it. Maybe it was from being sick all day. Or maybe it was from being upset with Sarah. But whatever it was, it really sparked a fire within him.

In his dream he was sick and in bed. Sarah had gone to get him some meicine. He had been sleeping and was feeling better when the bathroom door flew open and hit the wall. He sat up and looked to see Sarah standing with a dead baby goat. She held a knife in her hand and with it she cut its throat. Blood spilled out over its dead body and over her hand.

"This is all for you," she said with blank eyes. She lifted the dead goat over her head and let the blood fall over her long hair and body. "It is all for you," she said again as the blood ran down her neck.

"Sarah, what are you doing?"

"The stars Matthew, they are all pointing south. And it is all for you. It is all...for...YOU!" Sarah screamed and threw the dead baby goat at him.

Ther next morning when he had awoke, Matthew thought and thought about the dream. And what he thought about the most was the sound that the dead baby goat had made when it was thrown at him. It sounded like a word.

"Heroin," Mattehw said to himself.

He never told Sarah about the dream. Which was something that they both did quite often. It was always a good way to start the morning together.

What did you dream about?

No, you first.

No, YOU first. I insist.

But this one dream Mattehw would keep to himself. "She would think I had gone mad," he told himself.

There were a couple more days of methadone. But it died out fast. It just wasn't the same as heroiin. And since it was still unavailable, Sarah and Matthews next big venture would be Oxycontin. It was easier to get a hold of since it seemed to the both of them that everyone under the sun was high on it.

Matthew found that he liked the oxycontin pills better than the methadone pills. He and Sarah would crush the pills and snort them in one long rail. Even Carmen was involved, and the three of them would have what they called their OXY- Parties. A party with some friends where everyone was faded on those pills. It was a good time for Sarah and Matthew. But just like most things in life, it didn't last long. It never does.

24

To anyone who was invited to the house, and to anyone who might run into them on the street, Sarah and Matthew looked to be the perfect couple. An example of what a couple should be. They were always so close to each other. And they were always laughing and smiling. And it seemed to have an effect on those lucky people with whom they would meet and sometimes befriend.

Everyone talked about them. Even the parents of Sarah and Matthews friends knew about them. As was the case with Carmen. Her mother had come down from Georgia. And upon meeting the couple said: "Oh, I am so glad to finally meet you. I have heard so much about you both." And afterwards, gave them a hug.

Carmen that day was sick. You *could* say she was dope sick. But she had her own secrets that not even Sarah would ever know. And Carmen did her best to hide it. And she did for the most part. But a mothers instinct somehow *always* knows when her children have been playing with the wrong things.

Before Carmens mother had left, she gave her daughter a good and long lecture on the effects of drug use and too much partying. All of which made Carmen lie to her mother by telling her that she does not take drugs, and that the partying had gone down significantly since she broke up with her last boyfriend. And it was a single day after Carmen's mother had visited that it happened. Sarah and Matthews descent into hell went deeper. And bloodier.

25

It had started with a fight. Sarah had had too much to drink. And Matthew had taken one too many oxycontin pills. For Sarah's liking.

"YOU ARE GOING TO DIE FROM THAT STUFF!" Sarah yelled at him. "OR MAYBE THAT'S WHAT YOU WANT. YOU WANT TO DIE, DON'T YOU?"

"Sarah, just relax. Alright? You have had too much to drink and you are acting up. Just take it easy."

"DON'T TELL ME TO TAKE IT EASY!" Sarah shouted to him as she stood up with a bottle in her hand. It looked as though she wanted to hit him with it. Matthew, not in the least bit to put up with her attitude, dared her to do it.

"Go ahead. If it makes you feel better, hit me with it. Hit me as hard as you can. Maybe you will get lucky and you will cut my skin so deep that it can't be healed and I will die."

"Oh, don't give me that pity bullshit."   .

"I am not giving you anything, Sarah."

"Oh yeah, Matthew." Sarah took the beer bottle and broke it on the edge of the nightstand. Pieces of glass scattered onto the floor and onto the skull and roses. She turned and placed the busted bottle to Matthews throat.

"You are going to give me whatever I want. Because if ou don't, I am going to cut your throat," Sarah threatened him. Only Matthew didn't see it as that much of a threat. He actually *wanted* to be cut. And so did Sarah. But neither one of them could admit it to the other.

"Go ahead then Cut it," Matthew dared her.

"Stop daring me to do it bitch. Because I will miss you up."

"Either cut me or leave me the hell alone. I am not looking to fight with you. I love you too much to fight for no reason."

"Too bad bitch. I want a fight."

"PISS OFF, SARAH!"

Sarah was taken back a moment. But she gathered herself quickly and slapped Matthew so hard across his mouth that he bled. And seeing that he had taken those pills earlier, the slap wasn't as bad to him as it should have been.

Matthew's next move only made the anger between the two of them worse. He pushed her against the nightstand. Everything was knocked out of place. And the skull was turned over, revealing a little bag of white powder. Both Sarah and Matthew stood for a moment and looked at it. Then at each other. That old itchy feeling had consumed Matthew by now, and all he wanted to do was scratch his face and arms until he bled. But he didn't dare make a move.

Sarah grabbed the bag and held it out to him.

"What is this?" She asked while shaking the bag in his face. A face that was now half red from the slap he received. "Is this coke, Matthew?"

He only stood and looked at her. And once again, Sarah couldn't tell the expression on his face. She simply couldn't figure him out. And it made her more angry with him. And herself.

"What is this stuff? You had better answer me or you will get it," Sarah threatened.

Silence.

Matthew just stood and looked at her. Blood covered his lips and was now starting to run down to his chin. Sarah took a closer step to him. Her eyes were crazed and she was having a little trouble standing in place. Matthew took the bag from her and placed it in his pocket.

"Yes," he said while pushing her gently away from him. "It is coke."

And that was all it took. Sarah lost her temper and grabbed Matthew by his shirt and started swinging. She didn't really hit him much. She loved him. She just wanted to fight. And so Matthew gave her one.

He put a hand to her face and pushe as hard as he could. Sarah's head went back as well as her body. She tripped over her feet and ran into the wall behind her. The sound was loud enough for Carmen to come running into the room and see what was happening.

"PLEASE STOP!" Carmen yelled. She wanted to stop them herself but had taken too many pills and was feeling too dizzy to do anything. She just leaned againt the door and watched. She was at first terrified. It looked as if Sarah was being beaten. She was thrown around the room in all corners. But then at other times, it looked as though it was Matthew who was being beaten. Only, he wasn't thrown anywhere.

"This is just too confusing for me. I can't decide who to feel sorry for," Carmen tells them.

"Don't feel sorry for either of us. This is just a good time for us," Sarah tells her during one of their brief intermissions of the fight.

Carmen just couldn't believe what she had heard. That what her two friends were having was *fun*. And how was *that* supposed to be fun?

She was too high to figure the question. And she was cathing nods. Just like Sarah and Matthew had the night before. And Carmen had stopped eating like they had. And she had stopped working like they had. And she was taking too many drugs like they were. And as the fight went on, and as more blood was shed, Carmen would go back to her room and take more pills and smoke out of her pipe.

After the fighting had stopped, Sarah and Matthew lay next to each other on their bed. Beaten, bruised, and sore. They wouldn't speak. But they did look at each other and hold hands. And that was good. Especially after how hard they had fought each other. And of course, there was no winner. Both of them lost. They had both met their match. Oddly enough.

Sarah would wake the next morning with a black eye. She would also have several bruises on her arms and legs tat would take days to heal. Matthew would have bruises as well. But noi black eye. But he did have a busted lip, and they both had several severe scratches. All of which dried in a long thick scab.

Outside of their room, Carmen lay on the couch. She had taken too much and had tried to reach the bathroom sometime in the night. She never made it. Instead she had fallen to her knees next to the couch and was sick on the floor. She passed out soon after.

"Kiss me," Sarah said as she moved closer to Matthew. "Your lip is still bleeding butyou can kiss me anyway. I don't mind. I love you."

"Come here then."

Sarah moved close and they hugged and kissed. Sarah felt the blood over her lips and tasted it as it ran into her mouth. Matthew ran his hands over her bruised back and scratched arms. And as he did, he would feel the scabs and wondered just what in the hell had he done.

"You taste good, baby," Sarah told him after the kiss was done.

"I'm glad you like me."

They both smiled.

What happened next is something that can turn anyone's stomach. Especially those who have a low tolerance for the thought (or sight) of blood.

They had taken their clothes off and were exploring each others body. Something that they had done a million times before, only this time, and when Sarah looked over her mans body, she wanted to cry. She was sitting on top and looking down upon his pale and skinny body. A body that had once not been so skinny and pale. Nor was it physically damaged it is was now.

She leaned forward and gave him another long kiss. But before they would go any further, Matthew would ask for something. Something that he would want from her.

"Anything for you my love," she tells him. And Matthew could feel the sincerity in her voice. He could *see* it in her green eyes.

"Cut me while you love me. Okay?"

"Cut you?" Sarah asked. "With what."

Matthew reached over and picked up one of the pieces of broken glass that sat next to the skull and roses. He placed it in her hand.

"Alright my love," Sarah tells him.

That night, a full moon rose high in the south Florida sky. It shone its luminous light brightly upon their naked bodies as they slept side by side.

26

"Hello?" Sarah asked as she held the phone tightly in her hand. "Who is this again?"

She did not like the sound of the name that was given to her when she had answered. Matthew lay in bed asleep. It seemed that that was all they did these days. It had been too long since they had gone out.

"I am going to hang-up unless you tell me who you are."

"Its Chris. You remember me right?"

"Why are you calling me? I already told you that I have no time for you. There are millions of girls in the world, Chris, and for some reason you have to keep bothering me. So why don't you say what you have to and kick rocks. I am tired of hearing from you."

"I'm just calling to tell you that I am out now and that you *will* be seeing more of me. Because you are *my* girl and I own you. So get used to seeing a lot more of me."

"You own me. What a laugh," Sarah says with a hearty laugh. A laugh that ran on untl Chris hung-up the phone.

"I have something to tell you," she tells Matthew as he awakes. And at the end of it all, Matthew had one thing to say. It was a question.

"What do you want to do about him?"

"I don't know. Have any ideas?"

"Yes," Matthew says. "Yes I do."

27

"Our love is like a drug itself," Sarah said as they sat in Matthews car the following evening."But it also separates us when it wants too," she says quietly and sad.

Matthew only listened.

"And I don't think I can ever get off this drug. Not ever."

She leaned over and gave Matthew a kiss on the cheek. It was late this night. And they both sat in the Cruiser and waited. And what was it they were waiting for? They didn't even know. But whatever it was, tey both knew that it would be presented to them soon.

And so they waited at the end of the street that Chris lived on. Parked under a bunch of trees in the shadow of the south Florida night.

They waited for nearly an hour before Sarah finally said: "I wonder where his dog is? He always leaves it out at night."

And there was the answer. That one statement was exactly what Matthew had been waiting for. And he didn't waist a moments thought on what he wanted to do. He started the Cruiser and drove off.

"Where are we going?"

"To the nearest store. I have something to get. Ow are you sure he keeps that dog out at night."

Sarah said she was sure and that the dog was kept in a cage right outside the back door. It was a German Shepard. "A rather mean one too," she tells him as they pull into the parking lot of the nearest grocery store. "That dog is his whole life. His best friend."

"Well, that's good to know. I'll be back in a minute."

"Don't take too long. Okay, baby."

Matthew didn't.

Ten minutes later Matthew came back out with a plastic bag. Within this bag was a can of dog food and two brands of poison.

It was nearing two in the morning when Matthew pulled the Cruiser back into the same shaded place that he had before. They both sat a few minutes before sneaking their way behind the targeted house.

Sarah stood behind a bush while Matthew walked up to the cage. He had placed the poison in the canned food and held out in his hand. As soon as the dog saw him it began to growl. It showed its teeth and lowered its head in an act of attack. But Matthew was careful. There could be no mistakes.

Matthew could see a small opening that Chris pushed the dogs food through. Almost like isolation in a prison, Matthew thought. The dog continued to growl. And Matthew realized he was taking more time than he needed to.

He took a look behind him and saw Sarah standing behind the bushes and waving at him to hurry it up. So he placed the poisoned dog food through the small opening and backed away as fast as he could. The dog watched and growled. Louder this time. Matthew hid in a dark patch of shadow created by the corner of the house. He looked over at Sarah as she stood behind the bushes. Tnhey didn't speak. They just looked at each other, then at the dog. They both watched as the dog lowered his head and walked over to the canned food. There was a sick sort of excitement that they both felt as they watched the dog eat the poisoned food. They gave each other a smile. Sarah's green eyes seemed to glow through the dark. She giggled and held her hand to her mouth to silence herself.

It didn't take long for the dog to devour the poisoned food. And as soon as it had finished it began to gag violently. Its head jerked up and down. Its body shook. It fell over and was dead. Its head making a hard THUD as it hit the concrete floor. Matthew turned once again to see Sarah smiling back at him. Her eyes held that same sick excitement as Matthews. She made a motion for him to get moving and he held up his hand to tell her just one minute.

She looked at him with curiosity. She was expecting a fast getaway. But then she saw te pocketknife that Matthew pulled from his pocket. She was going to loose it. She shook and sweated with excitement. If she could, she would have ripped his clothes off right then and loved him tell the sun rose.

"Watch this," Matthew whispered to her.

He walked over to the cage. He quietly opened the cage door. He went inside. It never occurred to him to see if anyone else besides Sarah was watching. And to both their luck, no one was.

He approached the dead dog and knelt beside it. With the knife held firmly in his hand, he made a small cut along the ribs. The blood poured out faster than he could ever imagine. It ran a dark red over his hand.

Once done he walked out of the cage and back to the side of the building. He would leave a message for Chris. (One which was unreadable by sunrise). Then he and Sarah would go home as fast as they possibly could. Merrily laughing along the way.

28

Cocaine just wasn't working anymore. And it seemed that every time that they had a little, their enjoyment of the drug itself would turn into a feeling of sickness. As well as that uncomfortable feeling of having too much energy and not being able to find enough things to do to occupy their restless minds.

And it was on the same night that Matthew poisoned a certain someones dog that he purchased an eight ball. Most of it was cooked up and smoked. It was easy fo him to do. And he was surprised upon the discovery that Sarah had never bothered to cook her speed up herself. Never once in all the years that she had been taking the drug.

A little bit of this. And a little bit of that. And presto! Your good to go.

And of course it was after taking the drug that they had finally received that phone call that they had been waiting for. It was from their good friend Lindsey. She was calliong to inform them of a new and very reliable dealer. And that she had some heroin on her at that moment. And that two of the eggs were for the two of them to have at half the price. And that was even after she would give them a free sample.

"We are already high enough," Sarah had told Lindsey. "Can you wait till tomorrow to hook us up?"

Sarah asked this while rubbing her hand over her chest. It was hurting a little. But then again, after living off of speed for a few years, it is bound to catch up to a person.

Lindsey said that it was okay and hung up. Sarah set the phone down, but not back on the receiver. She wanted to be alone with her man. So she took off her shirt and pants and wore her red silk bra and panties. (Something that she knew Matthew had a great liking for. Even though it had never came up in any conversation).

"How do you feel, baby?" Sarah asked as she lay next to him on the bed. He had been quiet ever since coming home.

"Fine. But a little too high for my liking. I don't want to take this stuff again. It doesn't make me feel good anymore." He pauses for a moment before he speaks again. "It hasn't for a while now."

"I know what you mean. I wold much rather have some train. Or even some pills."

She ran her fingers through his hair. It was getting a litle long now. But not too long for her liking.

"Lets just get rid of the stuff that we have and start new tomorrow. Okay?"

"Sounds good to me," Matthew tells her.

Matthew lays over onto his side and falls asleep. Just something that he was able to do on speed while Sarah was not. And so she would watch televison. Or take more lines. Or write in her diary.

"I love you so much, Matthew," she tells him and kisses him on the cheek before leaving the room to see what show could possibly be on the tube. Nothing was. And so for the last time in her life, Sarah Blackwell sat uncomfortably on a couch and waited for the high of the speed that she had once loved so much, and had smoked an hour or so ago, to go down and disappear. And it did. Only it happened at sunrise when matthew and Carmen were getting up.

.   "Come lay down with me," Matthew told her. "I'll go back to sleep with you. I'm still tired and this is too early for me to get up anyway."

"Okay," Sarah told him. She was still wearing her red silk panties. As well as a t-shirt. Much to Matthew's relief.

They laid back in bed and loved each other for a while. Not as long as they usually go. Just long enough for the both of them to feel good. And afterwards, they fell asleep wrapped in the others arms as the sun rose high in the south Florida sky.

The world awoke as the two lovers slept. They wouldn't get up that day till the aternoon. After the working day was done for all those who *did* work. After the heat of the south Florida climate had gone down. And especially after Lindsey had called back about that little *something* that she wanted to share with the two of the.

"We'll be right over," Sarah told Lindsey after she had picked up on the sixth ring. "Matthew and I cannot wait to get hold of that stuff. So have it ready, okay."

"Okay, Sarah. No sweat," Lindsey assured her and hung up.

"Time to get up, baby."

But Matthew didn't get up. So she held him in her arms and kissed and licked him till he did. A little unusual, yes. But when you are in love like Sarah and Matthew are, then anything (as well as everything) is beautiful.

"Just give me a minute, okay?"

Sure thing, baby. Everythings going to be fine. Just fine," Sarah had promised. "The stars are pointing south tonight."

Matthew looked at her. A little wide eyed too. He had no idea why she would have said that to him since he had *never* told her about his dream.

"Why did you say that, Sarah?"

Sarah didn't answer. She only looked down at him with an emotionless expression. Her eyes piercing through his soul.

"Okay, I'm getting up."

And did this time.

29

He had forgotten how bad he used to itch on the *stuff.* He didn't know how Sarah felt. He never bothered to ask. He just knew she liked it as much as he did. And he had assumed that she got that itching feeling just like anyone else who fades on heroin.

It had always started with his nose. No matter if he snorted it or banged it. It was always the same. Start with the nose, then to his back and arms. He looked as though he were continually hugging himself while high. Good times, right?

"I want to have another line," Matthew told Lindsey as they stood next to one another in her apartment and watched everyone else as they took drugs and talked about nothing really important at all.

"Well then, come in here with me," Lindsey told him as she took his hand and lead him into the bathroom.

She had wanted to take him into her bedroom, but she knew that would have been one of the dumbest things that she could do. It was of no secrete that Sarah Blackwell was a jelous girl. And that she holds one of the worst tempers that a person can bare witness to.

And so with that knowledge already in tact within Lindsey's doped mind, she made two lines on the bathroom sink.

"Thanks a whole bunch for this, Lindsey."

"No problem, baby. Maybe you could help me out sometime, yeah?"

"Of course. Anytime."

Sarah and Matthew stayed at the party for another hour then left. They had only come for their *stuff.* And now it was time to go home. Which was wearing thin on them as well. They both felt that it was time to move on.

Matthew would be over with school soon. And so the small historic town of St. Augustine was the target.

Even though Matthew had given up working a steady job, he still attended classes when required to. And now that he was nearing the last few weeks, the need to get straight (just to move) was becoming a priority in his life. He realized fast that Sarah was going to expect him to make the decisions for the two of them. Which in a way made him feel better about the move. He liked to have that kind of control in his life.

Matthew would not take the both of them to a run down apartment, or house. He was better than that. As was she.

But for now, he would only think about the high and of Sarah. How beautiful she looked as she sat next to him in the car under the full moonlight. All the windows were down in the Cruiser, and the warm air blew in at a perfect temperature. It sent chills up and down his arm and back. It was one of those moments that he never wanted to end.

Before they went home, Matthew stopped at a local gas station and bought some snacks. Mainly chips, a few cans of Coca-Cola, and a whole bunch of chocolate. He was in the mood for something unhealthy. But so was Sarah. She had even made a small list of what kind of assorted chocolate he should get. And to get a *whole lot of it*, she had written.

She had also placed a p.s. at the bottom of the list that said: *If you think you have enough, then get more. Because chances are ... YOU DON'T.*

Matthew was in and out in less than five minutes. Much to Sarah's loking. She was feeling itchy. And was getting antsy. And wanted to be home already. She wanted to lay down and fade out. And she did. As well as Matthew. After the two of them snorted another bag each and felt that *burn* run down their nostrils. Then they were Dead In Heaven.

30

"I have found an apartment on Saragossa St. Do you know where it is?" Matthew asked Sarah when she had finally awoken after another long slumber. She acknowledged knowing the street and lit a cigarette. It caught Mattehw by surprise. He had never known her to smoke. But apparently she had in her past and had taken a few *cancer sticks* at the party the night before.

"I started again a week ago. I just miss it. That's all."

The 'it' that Sarah was referring to was nicotine. And quitting smoking was a lot harder for her to do than ending her love affair with cocaine. Which she happened to love a whole hell of a lot. She had just forgotten about it.

"Yeah, I know where Saragossa is. I grew up right around the corner from it. Well, not just around the corner," she said and laughed. Mattehw looked at her as if she had gone mad.

"Its not a bad deal. I already talked to the guy who we will be renting from and he has lowered the price from five hundred fifty to four hundred ninety five. He seemed really eager to get us in there. Probably since he already mentioned that he didn't care much for the people living there now."

"Sounds like your typical landlord, Matthew," Sarah says and takes another drag from her cigarette. "I'll call my mother tomorrow and tell her that we have a place and that we will be coming up there by the end of the month. Is that cool with you?"

"Sure."

But he wasn't really sure. He felt a little uneasy. Especially this morning. And with Sarah's attitude. She seemed distant and cold.

"Is everything alright?"

"Yeah, baby. I'm just a little tired is all. But the smokes are helping and I am ready to ride that train. But only if you are."

"Sure am." Matthew told her. "Lets fade out then," he said and cooked up an egg of heroin for her before one for him.

They went to the beach around noon. It was a little too hot for their taste. But the high, with the cool Atlantic water running across their feet, made it alright. And as soon as the high began to fade out itself, they would take more. Only instead of banging it, they would have to snort it. And nobody else on the beach that day noticed. And that's a good thing. Because Sarah and Matthew sat a few feet away from a mother and her children. The father had left for drinks, or maybe it was more towels. Matthew had wondered what would have happened if he and Sarah were to have been seen. But he was also irritated with the fact that the family was there to begin with.

He looked away quickly. He wanted more. He *needed* more. And he decided right then and there that they would buy and take with them so much heroin that they would vomit in ecstasy. And he also figured that there was no better time (or day) to get started than this one.

31

Carmen had been away for some time. She had mety up with another boy and had left with him to Panama City. Carmen hated it. She had gone to see if things between the two of them could work into something more serious. But things didn't. An she headed back to West Palm beach by means of Amtrak. She couldn't even remember how long it had taken to get from one city to the other. She was too high to know her own name when she had boarded. And to make her situation worse, she ended up sitting next to the snack bar and drinking Pepsi mixed with Vodka.

By the time the train pulled in at the West Palm station, Carmen had drank six drinks. And upon leaving the train, she ran right into the ladies room, fell to her knees, and was sick. Her habit's were getting worse all the time. And she knew it. But she couldn't stop. Or maybe it was she *wouldn't* stop. And she would often ask herself: *Would you if you had to make that choice?* And the answer to that question *always* came through a straw or syringe.

She had a good track line running up her arm. She had many bruises on her arms and legs. And she never could remember how they got there.

She didn't have enough money for a cab home, so Carmen had called Matthew for a ride. Which of course he did without hesitation. And when upon seeing her he thought: *My God, she looks worse than Sarah and I do.* But he would never say such a thing to her. That would have been rude and very inappropriate behavior.

They weree going to be leaving the Palm Beaches soon, and Sarah could hardly wait. Matthew had never been to the historic city. And so Sarah would tell him about it. She filled his head with all the little things that the city had to offer. She was very excited. And it made Matthew happy to see it. He knew how important it was for Sarah to go home and be with her family. Sher did miss them terribly. She had been talking to her sister and mother more frequently these days. Where as Matthew hardly ever talked to anyone from his.

And so it was on the last week of March that Sarah and Matthew, with Carmen, bought two hundred baggies of heroin. Ten in all. They were good sized bags. Enough to last all three of them the week out. (Which really happened because the three of them rationalized what they all had).

Sarah and Matthew had one syringe to share. Carmen had lost hers in Panama City, but had decided to just snort hers instead of replacing what she had lost. Which in return was the cause for her nose bleed by that Friday.

Sarah had thought of running Carmen to the emergency room by Saturday morning, but by the time that she was ready to go, Carmen informed her that the bleeding had stopped. All that was left was a bunch of dried blood and snot that stuffed her right nostril.

32

It had all started that Sunday. Sarah had a bit too much to drink and started a fight with Matthew. Just minutes before their friends came by to say their goodbyes to the couple. Neither Matthew nor Carmen knew why Sarah was acting up. The two of them figured it was because after spending a week Dead In Heaven, and now having to go without, that it was just the beginnings of her being dope sick.

But even then, Carmen knew that if Sarah and Matthew didn't get away from each other, and fast, that something bad would eventually happen. And that was when they received a phone call from Aallen. He was a local junkie. A bit off his head. But a good enough hook-up for anyone looking to score.

Matthew told Allen that he would be down to his place as soon as he possibly could. Carmen gave him money, as well as Sarah. Only, she pretty much threw the money at him with one of her death looks. That look of disgust that he had seen so many times before after Sarah had had too much to drink.

Matthew had told her once that she didn't need alcohol. And Sarah had agreed and even promised that she would stop. But she continued. And she had apologized four times already for her obnoxious behavior.

"How many times are you going to put up with it?" Lindsey asked Matthew after baring witness to Sarah's drunken rage one night.

"Until one of us kills the other."

That response made Lindsey see Matthew in a whole new perspective.

"You are not the person I thought you were," Lindsey told him.

Matthew only shrugged it off. He didn't care a bit for what anybody thought about him. Only Sarah. She was his life now. As he was hers.

"Come on in, Matthew," Allen said as he stood by the front door to his apartment. Matthew really didn't want to go in. Matthew had always hated going into *any* dealers home. It was never a smart idea. But luckily for him, he only had to be in there maybe three munites.

"Do you want to get fixed before you go?" Allen asked. He was even gross to look at. Hair not washed in months. Dark bags under his eyes (which were yellow, *yellow* I tell ya'), and ribs to be seen through his pale sweaty skin. Allen made Matthew feel sick to his stomach.

"No man. I'm cool."

Matthew left Allen's pad faster than he has ever left anyone's home. Allen laid on his couch as Matthew drove away. Allen faded into the afternoon. Pale, sick, and dying. He spent the rest of that day on that old used couch that he found out by the dumpster. He faded back into that dark place that he often visited while high on heroin. Allen and Matthew would never speak top each other again.

When Matthew got back to the house, Sarah was feeling rather guilty for her attitude earlier. And for that, *she* made love to him before making love to her other affair. They did that during the last hour of the party given to them by their friends.

"I want to bang this shit so bad that it hurts," Sarah said to both Matthew and Carmen. The three were sitting at the kitchen table. Matthew had taken the duty of cooking up the dope while Carmen snorted hers in one long rail. But to just sit and watch as Matthew cooked the drug made Carmen a bit edgy. She had never wanted a *stick* so bad.

"You first my darling," Matthew tells Sarah.

"Why thank you, baby."

The needle went smoothly into Sarah's vein. The drug ran out of the syringe warm and she felt that euphoric effect almost immediately. The world was at peace with *her* now. Matthew and Carmen's peace would come soon enough. Only, Carmen didn't see heroin in that way. To her, it was just fun. It had nothing to do with love or a way of life. Even though it *was* her life rather she acknowledged that truth or not.

Line after line and shot after shot, the three of them spent the last few hours together lost and 'Dead In Heaven'. No one ever wanting the experience to end. They slept little and ate less. They had partied all night and day that week. And now, by this Sunday, Sarah and Matthew would be up for two days straight. Matthew has bruises from puncture wounds running up his left arm. The same arm that had bled and bruised terribly after he carelessly left a syringe in one late night so long ago.

But they were having fun. With the drug (or at times *drug's*). And that's all that mattered.

By that Friday morning, Sarah looked used up. She had bite marks on her neck and stomach. She hadn't showered in three days, and as a result hadn't shaved either. She had cut marks around her breasts and thighs as well. And she was running a good track on her arm. Nicely long and scabbed.

"Just take this one hit with me and then we'll be done," Matthew told her as they continued to sit at the kitchen table.

Sarah took the syringe on emore time into her arm. She felt an instant rush of diziness, and fell to the floor. She passed out shortly after. She awoke in the bathroom in the shower with ice cold water running over her. She, as well as Matthew would never know just how close she had come to dying.

33

They awoke early Monday morning after receiving a phone call. It was fom Chris. Matthew had been the one who had answered he phone. He was told that he would pay for what he had done to his dog and for stealing *his* woman.

Matthew had denied any wrong doing in both matters and had even told Chris that he had no right to accuse him.

"I know you did it bitch," Chris says, "and I am gong to get you for it."

Matthew hung up and thought about what he had just been told. Did he really believe that he was going to let this *boy* get the best of him? No he didn't. And did he want Sarah to know what he was going to do about it? No he didn't.

And so it was the very next day that it all went down between Matthew and Chris.

"I am going out for awhile."

"When will you be back?" Sarah asked while being covered by the blankets. She looked at Matthew with a certain kind of unease. She did not want him to leave, but let him go regardless.

"Soon," Matthew tells her and walks out the bedroom and out the house.

Matthew had left the house around one that afternoon and had come back at eight that evening. He had a black eye and his knuckles were bloody. But that was all.

Twenty miles south, Chris sat on his mothers couch in *her* house and tried to accept the terrible truth that he had just received one hell of an ass-kicking. And not only that, it had happened right in his mothers front yard in daylight and with the neighbors all there to see.

"Where were you?" Sarah asked Matthew concernedly. She had taken out a warm washcloth and held it to Matthew's black eye. "I was so worried."

"No worries, baby. I just needed to take care os something."

He never told her what it was, but Sarah always knew.

34

St. Augustine, Florida.

The move to the historic city was a rather painful experience. Sarah and Matthew both became dope sick. And once again, they would have to cope without the drug unitl they could come across another dealer. And luckily for them, they didn't have to wait long.

The apartment on Saragossa St. was less than what Matthew had been told. First off, the location was wrong. He had been told by the landlord that the balcony view overlooked a cemetery (the same cemetery from which Sarah had gone into late one night and had dug up the skull that had been placed on her nightstand). The second thing wrong was that it was located behind the house. And the third thing was the noise. Both Sarah and Matthew had issues with people who played loud music. Neither one of them understood the whole concept behind it.

"Obviously anyone who plays their music really loud is gong to get a complaint," Sarah said after the two of them had moved in and had the unpleasant privilige of having to hear the downstairs neighbors blasting their stereo.

But the deal was done. And the two of them would be in that apartment for an entire year.

35

Their first meeting was less than pleasant. Sarah had brought Matthew to her home to meet the family. The old Victorian house sat two blocks away from the two lovers apartment. Sarah was more than excited to be going home.

She had decided it would be best to walk to the house. That way Sarah could tell Mttehw all about the city and some of her happiest memories. And it was upon passing the graveyard (that would have been in view if they had acquired the right apartment), that Sarah got quiet as they walked by.

Matthew didn't say anything. He didn't wan to. For he knew that there was a reason for nher silence and so he held her hand and walked in silence with her.

"Well, come on in, Sarah," Joyce said to her daughter as she opened the door. She gave her eldest daughter a kiss on her cheek and a hug. "And who is this young man?"

Sarah's mother was trying her best to hide her dissapointment. Not just for Matthew, but for Sarah as well. You see, the Sarah that had left St. Augustine was *not* the same Sarah that stood in her mothers hallway. She was a pale and skinny girl. Her hair was dirty and tangled. And she had horrible bags under her eyes.

And scars. SCARS. No, not my *daughter. Not my daughter.*

But it was true. And as much as Joyce didn't want to admit it, her daughter had a scar on her arm. Both of them. The scars both ran from her wrists on up to the pit of her skinny pale arms. And as Joyce followed the scar on one of her daughters arms, she also noticed the puncture marks around her daughters vein. But she would not say a thing.

Yet.

"Mom, this is Matthew. The love of my life."

"Well, it is a pleasure to meet you, Matthew."

"Thank you. It is a pleasure to meet You," Matthew responds with a hand shake. "I really like your home."

"Why thank you, Matthew," Joyce said with the sincerest tone that she could come out with. *Enjoy iy while you can* boy, *because you will* never *set foot in here again.* "Why don't you two go make yourselves comfortable and stay for awhile."

But even though they were offered to stay a while, there evening was cut short. Due to being so dope sick. They tried their best to hide it. But it was of no use. Joyce was too smart a woman to not notice. And Sarah's younger sister had even made a remark to the both of them after coming home from her field hockey practice.

"Wow, you guys look terrible," Jennifer said with a look of utter shock. "You guys musy be really sick."

"Gee, thanks," Sarah says sarcastically.

"Go on up stairs honey. I will be up there in a minute," Joyce tells her youngest daughter. And off she went. Light as a feather she ran up the stairs and into her bedroom before heading into the bathroom and taking another of her long showers.

Sarah and Matthew spent a few more minutes telling Joyce about their experience doen in the Palm Beaches. And Joyce listened patiently with her hands resting on her crossed legs. She had made a cup of tea and had only taken a sip from it. She was so angry at Sarah for how she had turned out. And for bringing Mathew to her house. He was *not* what she had imagined.

"Sounds very exciting. I should go down there sometime," Joyce tells them.

"You should mom," Sarah says while trying her best to not get sick. "Listen, we have to get going. We are both very tired and need to get some rest for tomorrow."

"Of course, Sarah. I understand," Joyce said to her dope sick daughter. She sat up from her favorite chair and led Sarah and Matthew to the front door.

"Call me tomorrow if you like. Okay darling?"

"Okay. I will," Sarah says and gives her mother a kiss on the cheek.

Joyce gives her daughter a hug and could not help but feel how thin her eldest daughter has become.

"See you later," Sarah calls out as she and Matthew walk down the sidewalk.

"Goodbye, Sarah. And to you as well, Matthew. It was nice to have met you."

Joyce was trying now. *Really* trying to keep it *cool* herself.

"Thank you," Matthew calls back. It was the only thing he could think to say. He knew he was not welcome here. E was no dummy. He knew it as soon as he saw the look on Joyce's face.

"Goodbye, Matthew," Joyce said again, only so that no one could hear her. She closed the front door quietly. She had wanted very badly to SLAM the damn thing. But she did not want to cause alarm with Jennifer or to let Sarah know just how pissed she really was.

36

After leaving her mothers house, Sarah took Matthew to one of the many bars that occupy the downtown streets of St. Augustine. Matthew didn't drink, but Sarah did. And it was while sitting there that Matthew would acquire his new job as the bars new prep cook/dishwasher.

"How utterly exciting this will be for me," Matthew tells Sarah after talking to the kitchen mamnger of the joint. His sarcasm wasn't missed, even by an inch. "I start this weekend."

"Well its money," Sarah tells him in hopes that he would cheer up. Sh was already on her third beer and wanted more. Matthew would have told her no, but he wasn't buying and so he knew it would be in his best interest to keep his mouth shut.

"If we could only find a hook-up we'll be set."

"We will, Matthew. It might take some calls for me to find out who's still around. I'll start with my goth friend and see if she knows anyone."

"Can you call her tonight?"

"No. She wouldn't like that too much. Like I said, she's a goth and so she's very moody. You know how *those* people are."

"Yeah I do. Unfortunatly."

About an hour later (as well as eight beers) a man named Rainbow Jack appeared. He was one of the locals and just happened to specialize in hallucinogenic. Which was not at all what Sarah and Matthew were looking to get into. But Rainbow jack knew a guy who knew *another* guy who sold enough heroin to supply the entire city of St. Augustine.

"So, when do you guys want to party?" Rainbow Jack asked. He was wearing a Grateful Dead t-shirt, dirty blue jeans, and an old pair of Nikes. He looked as thogh he hadn't showered in a week and was accompanied by an unwanted smell.

"How about tomorrow?" Sarah asked.

Matthew stayed quiet and to himself. He didn't care at this point if they had *it* tonight or later in the week. He actually didn't even want to be bothered with the whole thing.

"That sounds fine with me. I would rather leave the stuff alone tonight. I'm in a drinkin mood," Rainbow Jack says and holds his glass of beer up in the air. Sarah held hers up and Matthew held his glass of soda. The three made a toast and clinked their glasses together.

"To new friends and beginnings," Rainbow Jack said cheerily.

Sarah and Matthew smiled and drank.

Sarah finished her final beer, went to the ladies room, and came back to get Matthew so they could go home. He was waiting patiently for her while Rainbow Jack talked to him about a bunch of nonsense. Matthew was more than happy to see her come back and take his hand.

"It was very nice to have met you," Sarah says to Rainbow Jack. Matthew didn't say anything. He was still being shy.

"Well, it was very nice to have met the both of you. *Especially* you, Sarah." Jack looked her body from head to toe, then back to her dark green eyes.

"Well thank you. Come on baby."

"Talk to you guys tomorrow!"

Sarah turned and gave Rainbow Jack a friendly wave and smile. It warmed him to see it. After all, Sarah could make *any* mans heart melt with that smile of hers. But as soon as she and Matthew were out of the bar, she says: "What an unbelievable creep. He is damn sure lucky that he is helping us in scoring some train, because if he were some random guy, I would have smacked him right then and there when he made that pass at me, then checked me out."

"We should be real careful not to get too close to him," Matthew eplied.

They held hands as they walked down Cordova street. They were only three blocks from where the apartment was. And as soon as they arrived home, they both fell fast asleep.

It was almost as if they were back, living in the Palm beaches. Only in a much nicer place. They held each other while they slept. They were lost in each others love for one another. They both thought that a new life was ahead of them. A *better* one at that. But neither Sarah or Matthew knew just how soon their life together in St. Augustine would end.

37

Rainbow Jack sat on a bench under the Bridge of Lions and looked out upon the running water of the Matanzas River flowing by. He looked far down, towards the old fort. He was awaiting the arrival of his new friends. They were late and he was slowly getting irritated. He was beginning to believe that Sarah and Matthew were not serious about the purchase. And that was one thing that would always make Rainbow Jack loose *his* cool. He thought it was an insult to stand him up. Especially when it came to the purchase of drugs.

And it was right at the time when Rainbow Jack was getting ready to make his leave that Sarah and Matthew finally showed up. They looked used up. And Rainbow Jack wondered if the two of them had already banged some up before showing up.

"Alright, lets get on with it. I need to feel better and get home. That okay with you, Jack?" Sarah asked.

"Sure," he replied. Rainbow jack could tell that Sarah was no girl that he wanted to piss off.

"I have a hundred on me," Matthew says, "do you have any train on you or do we need to go somewhere?"

"I thought that I would meet you guys here, then go over to my place. Its just over the bridge. I know, I know, a motel isn't the perttiest place to make a home. But it sure is cheap as hell."

Matthew said it was fine, but he couldn't help but notice how tight Sarah squeezed his hand upon saying those words.

"Oh, its cool you guys. My friend is going to meet us there. He's probably there right now. Let me give him a call."

And so Rainbow Jack called his friend, Tom, who was sitting right by the door to Rainbow Jacks motel room while drinking an ice tea. Tea always helped Toms gum decay. It cooled his gums a good bit since that was all he had to work with since loosing *all* of his teeth. Which is a matter that till this very day has remained a mystery.

"Yeah, he's there. So we should get to steppin if you guys want some stuff," Rainbow Jack suggested. He reminded Sarah of Beavis from *Beavis and Butthead*. Only older and with orange skin.

Sarah and Matthew stood in silence as they looked at Rainbow Jack. Neither one knew what to do next. So they waited for him to start the move across the bridge and into St. Augustine beach... and heaven.

A few blocks away, Joyce was leaving a note for Sarah by setting it between the front and screen door. It was a note for Sarah to call her as soon as she got back. She had a plan to get her daughter away from Matthew. She had called a counselor who worked with addicts and had asked in help with an intervention. The counselor agreed.

"Oh thank you so very much, Diane. You have no idea how much my daughters new life is affecting me right now. You see, she is with this boy, and he is no good to her."

"Well, don't you worry, Joyce," Diane the counselor assured her, "we'll get your Sarah away from him. Its just one of the things that we do."

Joyce and Diane the counselor said there goodbyes and hung-up the phones. Afterwards, Joyce would go to Sarah and Matthews apartment with a note for her daughter to call her, before going back home and having a sip of hot tea while sitting in her chair. She needed to relax. She did not want Jennifer to see her upset when she came home from school.

Matthew never believed that he would ever see anyone more disgusting than Allen, but upon looking at Tom, he knew that *now* he would never see anyone more disgusting. Tom *is* toothless. But his gums are rotted with black and yellow spots, just like Matthews good friend Snowflake. And Tom carried an even more disgusting tan. More so than Allen ever would. All due to Tom's daytime job as an construction worker.

"I don't know why we just didn't drive over." Sarah said irritably. That way we could have stayed in the car and drove around the block."

"I thought it was too nice a day to drive. That's all," Matthew told her as they stood behind Rainbow Jack.

"I guess we can do that," Tom told Rainbow Jack. "But give me a few. Okay?"

"Sure thing, Tom."

And off Tom went atound the corner himself. Sarah and Matthew were both getting a little nervous about the whole deal. They both looked at each other with an expression that said: We should get outta here. Kick rocks. Scram!

But then Tom came back just as soon as he had left. And the two lovers eased up a bit. Tom came up to them and shook Sarah's and. As he did, the four eggs of heroin fell into her hand, then he let go. He shook hands with Matthew and received the forty dollars, then it was all over. Off Sarah and Matthew went. They didn't even tell Rainbow Jack or Tom goodbye. They just made like a tree and split.

"Nice couple," Tom said to Rainbow Jack as they watched them leave.

"Yeah. And that's one hell of a woman. She would fit so nice in my crib. And that would be just fine. Mighty fine indeed."

"Man, you'll never have a woman in your dirty, stinky, crib. So just *you* forget about all *that*."

"Whatever you say," Rainbow Jack tell Tom and gives him smile. "Lets go buy you some teeth."

They both laughed. And they both left together and went to one of the many bars of St. Augustine beach.

38

Before heading back to the apartmentm Sarah and Matthew stopped at the local pharmacy. Sarah went in since she was wearing the ony short sleeved shirt this day.

She made her way easily and calmly to the back counter and asked for a syringe for her B12 shot. She told the lady working on the other side of the clean, white counter that she had recently moved back and had lost her prescriptions and *supplies*.

The lady at the counter looked at Sarah's arms and asked what the red marks running up from her wrists were all about. Sarah told the lady that the marks were the result of an auto accident. And that the accident was the reason for her coming home. There was a moment of silence as the lady behind the clean, white counter looked at her. But Sarah never broke her cool. She stayed just as calm and collected as a murderer on trial who is trying to convince the jury that he didn't do it. The lady behind the clean, white counter finally reached under the counter, took out a single wrapped syringe, then sold it to Sarah.

Sarah left as fast as she could.

39

She did it before going over to her mothers. She banged two eggs befoe Matthew did the other two. But by the time that Matthew did his, Sarah was gone. She walked over to her mothers. She hadn't driven since moving back, which was probably for the better. Especially now. For Sarah Blackwell was *very* high.

The walk over was euphoric n itself. Sarah felt as though she didn't even have to be Dead In Heaven to be in the state that she was in now. The air was cool. And the sun shone warm onto her pale face.

She stopped in front of the cemetery that she had visited one night so long ago. She looked to the old oak tree that bent forward and covered the rear corner of the burial site. Its king arms overshadowed one grave in particular. And it was this grave that Sarah had dug into and taken the only thing that seemed reasonable to take.

A skull.

It laid in that dark muddy hole at the head of decaying bones. The nigh that Sarah had dug this grave, she had four lines of coke and half a bottle of whiskey. To say the least, she did not remember much about it. And she felt something terrible the next morning. Mainly throughout her head.

It all seemed like a dream. A dream that she could *still* feel now. Even while standing at the steel fence and looking in and upon this old historic cemetery as the sun settled into the western sky.

I have tto tell him. But I'm afraid.

She wanted so very badly to tell Matthew the story and *why* she had commited the act of grave robbing. But she was too afraid of what Mathew's reaction would be. What if he leaved her? Or what if he called the cops?

That would never happen. Are you kidding?

Sarah felt chills run up her arms as the cool wind picked up. It was oddly cold for this time mof year. Even with fall just around the corner. There was a tour group walking her way. And Sarah did not want to be anywhere near those people when they came to her spot. So she made haste and went to her mothers house.

"Are you using, Sarah?" Joyce asked as the two of them sat at the kitchen table.

"No. I'm not using," Sarah answered s she scratched at her nose and side of her pale face. "I promise you. I'm clean."

Knowing that her daughter was lying to her only angered Joyce more. She did not raise her daughters to lie. And her increased anger made Joyce want to smack the taste out of Sarah's moouth.

"How about Matthew?"

"You don't know what your talking about. We drink, that's all."

"I know you are lying to me. And I know that that boy your with is the reason that you are the way you are now."

"YOU DON'T KNOW SHIT!" Sarah screams. Her pale face was now a bright red. Joyce jumped a little at the sound of her daughters high pitched voice. "You don't know anything. So just stay out of it."

"I know that you are messed up and that I am going to fix it. And you better believe your sweet little ass that I mean every word that is coming out of my mouth," Joyce tells Sarah calmly. She would not give in to any of Sarah's games or her temper.

"I'm ..." Sarah began.

"I'm not going to argur with you about this. I love you so much, Sarah. And I will do whatever I have to just to make sure that you and Jennifer are alright in this world. So don't think for an instance that you canlie to your mother and get away with it."

There was a moments silence while Joyce waited for Sarah to respond.

"I'm going to leave now," Sarah tells Joyce, "I guess I will see you around. But before I go, I would advise that you not interfere with my business again. That's if you still want to speak to me again."

Trying very hard not to yell or grab her daughter Joyce said, "Okay. I am going to leave you alone and let you go about your own business. I njust hope you don't forget me. Or you sister. She needs you. You may not know that or believe it, but she does. Okay?"

Sarah didn't want a guilt trip. And so she told her mother goodbye and walked out of her mothers house. She didn't go home just yet. She wanted too. Because she really needed to be with her man right now. But she also needed time to herself. If only for a little while.

40

Matthew sat at the top of the wooden staircase that ran up to the front door of the apartment. He was leaning against the wooden rail and was fading in and out. He thought that everything was going to be fine. He really did. But then again, whoever he wasn't sober, *everything* was just fine and dandy.

The staircase was old and rotting. And worse than that, it was painted a light blue. A light blue that was peeling off in all the wrong places. And when Matthew had stood up, he found blue chippings on his shoulder and his dirty brown hair. He hated it here. And he could feel that uncomfortable feeling that he had *been* feeling since their arrival into the city.

Something isn't right here.

He held his hand to his stomach.

Why isn't Sarah back yet? Whats happened to her? Whats happened to you?

"Whats happened to us?" Matthew asked aloud. But not so loud that anyone could hear. Not that anyone was around anyway.

Matthew went inside and tried to eat. It didn't do much for him. He only found himself curled up in bed and feeling cold and shaking. Sarah came home hours later and wouldn't say where she had been. But Matthew had a pretty good guess. The smell of alcohol on her breathe gave it all away. She had decided to tell Matthew the story behind the skull. No matter what the outcome would be, she would tell him. And since he was already in bed, and sick, she figured now was the best as any to reveal the big secret.

"Very interesting," Matthew told her after she had finished her story. He gave her a kiss on the cheek, got out the bed, ran into the bathroom, and was sick. Sarah was left in the room wondering if it was the cause of the dope that made him sick or the story. She figured it best to leave him alone.

41

About a month had gone by now. Sarah and Matthew were fading out everyday now. Even as she sat in her mothers house, she was fading out. Well, trying her best not to.

"The end is only the beginning," Joyce told her. "And if you agree to enter this program yo will *not* be abl to leave. Because if you do, then you will serve the remaining time in jail."

Sarah looked at her mother, then over at Diane the counselor. And by the look that Sarah gave *her*, she became very nervous and looked down at the floor. This was one of the hardest things that she had to go through. She had known Sarah Blackwell for quite a while. And she had nearly cried upon the site of her.

"So either way I'm going to be taken into custody, right?" Sarah asked, but only looking at her mother. Joyce only looked at her daughter. It was Diane the couselor who had answered. And the answer was yes. Because Sarah was high and carrying, then that was enough for her mother to have that police car sitting outside and waiting.

"Then let me call matthew and let him know what is happening. I at least deserve the right to do that. Even if *you* don't like him," Sarah tells her mother with a stern look.

"You can call him when you go to the Home. (Which is the name of the recovery house that Sarah has been given the choice of going to).

"Well, mother. I want to call him now."

"Well, daughter. I am telloing you that you will *not* call him from here."

And it was at this point that Sarah got up and walked out of her mothers house.

42

It was four hours later that Matthew heard from Sarah. She had said that she would be gone half an hour. And that half hour was a long time ago. So to get that phone call and to know that she wasn't hurt was very relieving to hear.

But even at the relief of knowing that his love wasn't hurt, he still had to endure the pain of not having her with him this night. Or the next two to three months. She had been arrested. For narcotics possession and under the influence.

"SHIT!" Matthew yelled into the phone.

"I'll get out, baby. I promise," Sarah told hin with a shaky voice. She was scared. She hated making Matthew mad. She wanted to cry. But she wouldn't. Not while in jail.

"when will that be?" Matthew asked nervously.His hand was shaking badly and he wanted to be sick. "Please tell me that you are joking and that you are going to come home in five minutes. Maybe even less. Please tell me that. PLEASE!"

"Matthew, I love you so much that it makes me want to cry. I love you so much that it is hurting my stomach. And all I want to do is leave this place and come home. But I can't. And before you say it, you can not come see me. Because *they* know who you are and I know tha twe have been watched. So just clean up and stay away from Jack and anybody else who associates with him."

"That's fine. But how am I going to stay calm without you?"

"Just wait for me. Wait for my calls, and read my letters. Because I am not going to lose you. Not like this."

There was a moment of uncomfortable silence. All that could be heard now was the slow breathe taken in and out from the both of them. Waiting for someone to speak. And it was finally Sarah who said that she had to go.

"Please Sarah, don't. Don't leave me here in this place alone. I can't stand the thought of being without you."

"But I have to, baby. I don't have a choice. I'm in jail."

"I love you Sarah. Don't forget that. Ever."

"I love you too. And always will," Sarah tells Matthew and feels the tears running down her cheeks. But she wouldn't let it out. Not in here. Not now.

"Bye for now, baby," Sarah tells Matthew.

"Sarah wait..." he says but it was too late. Sarah was gone. And now Matthew was left alone in a darkened apartment that seemed to have become darker now as he sat alone. Sarah was gone. And within minutes he would be gone too. Matthew dropped the phone onto the floor, blocked out that annoying *beeping* sound that comes when the phone is off the hook, cooked the rest of his heroin, and stuck it in his arm without a care in the world.

Matthew was Dead In Heaven.

43

Sarah was sentenced to serve a year in jail with six months suspended. All due to the amount of heroin with which Sarah had on her at the time. And with the way the drug was bagged, it did not in any way help her case.

Jennifer had a friend who lived on Saragossa St. and who kept an eye out on Matthew and his living habits while he was still there. It was fun for her. It made her feel like a detective.

Sarah was released from ajil on a Friday morning. She was happy for her release and for being clean. But as happy as she was, she was still filled with sadness and anger for knowing that in the end, Matt hew had become tired of her absence and left.

She cried as she stood at the foot of the staircase that led to what was once there home. She remembered how excited she was when she and Matthew first walked those steps and into their home. How he held her and kissed her. But her memory and sadness faded away as her anger once again reappeared.

She had to find Matthew. She had to have him back and to know why he had left. The *real* reason. They wrote. And she called him. But then came that one letter that said he was leaving. Going back to the Palm Beaches.

She walked over to the bar of which Matthew previously worked. The kitchen maneger said that matthew had left a month earlier. Headed back to West Palm Beach. He wasn't sure what day. And that didn't matter. She at least knew where to find him. And she was planning on doing just that as sson as she could get away from her mother and St. Augustine.

On the day that she left, Sarah went home and pulled out the box of letters that was received from Matthew while her stay in jail. She packed them into her book-bag, along with other necessities. Her other bags were already in the car and waiting.

"I'm going out for a while. Okay with you?" Sarah asked her mother. "I won't be long. I just need to get a job and get back into the swing of things."

"Alright then..." Joyce began, "just please..."

"I know, mom. Everythings going to be fine. Don't worry," Sarah says with a smile.

"I know, Sarah. But its my job to worry. Please don't hold that against me."

"I don't. And I understand. I don't think I ever told you, but thanks for all that you have done for me. It really means a lot." And even though Sarah was giving her mother love, she still felt the anger of loosing her freedom because of her. And her man.

"I love you, Sarah," Joyce told her eldest daughter for the last time. Only she didn't know that this would be the last time that she would ever speak to her.

"I love you too, mom. See you later."

And out the door Sarah went. The trunk of her BMW stuffed with her luggage. The car floor on the passenger side filled with food and drink. It still took a while to get the car heated. Which made the situation a little more uncomfortable. And she could hardly contian her composure. And sh knew that while she was sitting in her car and waiting, her mother was watching from inside.

"Come on damnit! Lets go!"

Yes, Sarah was getting to the point of yelling at the car now. It had been minutes. Maybe close to fifteen by now. And the afternoon was fading fast. She wanted to get into West Palm by no later than eight that night. But by the looks of things, that didn't seem likely.

Finally, after he cars engine had settled and the temp gauge was in its proper place, Sarah Blackwell left home. She would never know it, but as she pulled away, her mother had walked out to tell her something of great importance. But instead, she was left standing at the foot of her walkway watching her daughter drive away from her.

44

She drove fast down the interstate. Almost too fast. There was no music playing. And there was no smile on her face. She had called Carmen after leaving St. Johns county. She wasn't even sure if Carmen would answer. Or if she even lived at the house. But to Sarah's relief Carmen answered and all was good.

"Yes, I have seen him," Carmen told Sarah. "But I don't know where he is staying at the moment. But I am so happy to her from you though. I have missed you both so very much."

"I have missed you too."

But truth be told, Sarah didn't miss Carmen in the least bit. She could only think of Matthew. And what was going to happen when she saw him again. She could feel the butterflies in her stomach as she thought about him. It made her sick. She put a cigarette between her lips and held it there till the cars lighter was ready. Her hand shook as she stabbed the cancer stick into the mouth of the cars lighter.

By the time that she pulled into the driveway to the house in Jupiter it was nearing eleven thirty.

The room that she and Matthew stayed in was now occupied by another couple. But it just wasn't the same Carmen had told her. She had also said that the main reason for her letting the new couple stay was to fill the void that was felt after Sarah and Matthew had left and moved up north.

"There named are Steve and pam. They came down from some small town in Georgia. Can you believe that, Sarah? They are nothing more than two backwoods hicks from Georgia." Carnmen thought this funny and had a good laugh about it. It wasn't at all funny. But with the pills that Carmen was taking (and had even shared with Sarah), the entire world was funny.

"So, you really don't know where Matthew is?"

"No babe. He was around at first, but..."

"But what?"

"I don't know. You see, he's real secretive. Like, he doesn't say much or even answer questions when asked."

Something about what Carmen had said made Sarah curious. Carmen seemed nervous. As if she was lying and knew something that she didn't want Sarah to know.

"So you know nothing?" Sarah asked.

"I can tell you that he goes to the beach. Way more than he used to. And he looks real good. In fact, he looks *really* good."

And it was at this moment that Sarah realized Carmen knew more than she was telling. Carmen knew exactly where to find Matthew. She just didn't want Sarah to know. And the thought of Carmen chasing after Matthew made Sarah sick to her stomach. And it made her mad as hell. But a much as she wanted o hurt Carmen, she had to stay calm. She had to keep her cool.

At least for now. Sarah thinks. But she must be careful. She cannot let her emotions get the best of her.

Later that night while on the couch, Sarah thought about the past. All those months here with Matthew. All the good times and bad. And Carmen. She thought about her and when exactly did that little bitch start to have feelings for *her* man.

She laid on her back. She couldn't sleep. But she really didn't want to. She wanted to go out and find Matthew. And she would have gone but not knowing where he was, well...

She stayed awake till her eyes were so heavy that they refused to stay open. She fell asleep while remembering the first time she and Matthew had made love.

That first week came and went. And then the second and the third. Sarah had picked up work at a local bar. She waited tables some nights and bartended on others. She was hit on by more men than she could ever imagine. She was looking better. Her tan was back, her hair was nice and long, and her figure was full and as beautiful as ever. Just like it had been when she and Matthew first started to see each other.

Her scars didn't even show. (Well, not the old ones). Sarah had become so obsessed with the thought of her and Matthew together that she cut his name was a razor on her stomach. It was the only way for her to settle her nerves.

She made new friends. And she was invited to parties and to go out. And that was good for her. Just as long as everyone knew that she was in no way of seeing anyone. Which her new friends were fine with. They were just happy to have her friendship. Just as anyone would be if given the chance to be with her.

By the fourth week she had started to give up hope of ever finding her man. It had been months. MONTHS! And it was when she had given up on her search that she found him. He was sitting alone and staring out into the Atlantic late one afternoon.

She had gone to Juno beach not in hopes of finding him, but more of herself. She never noticed the grey PT Cruiser sitting at the end of the lot.

She stood for a moment and looked at him. She was nervous. And all the things that she had planned on saying to him vanished from her mind at the sight of him. But none of it mattered anyway. He was there. And so was she. And everything was beautiful. Once again so beautiful.

She walked over to him.

45

They didn't speak. They just held hands for a long time and looked into each others eyes. Matthew had been startled at first. It was as if he was broken out of some dream when Sarah sat down next to him. She had wanted to know what he was thinking, but then found herself unable to say a single word.

The sun was setting and darkness covered the ocean sky. The breeze was cool and the water cooler. And it was Matthew who finally broke the silence:

"You looking for a boyfriend?"

"Depends," Sarah said as she looked into his eyes. "You looking for a girlfriend?"

The sun set and the moon rose as they held each other tight in each others arms.

December 13, 1974

1

When she had heard the words that YES, she was pregnant, she couldn't have imagined that she could feel any happier. But then, when she had heard the news that the new addition to the family was going to be a boy, she knew that *then*, was without a doubt, the happiest she could feel while sitting on that chair within that all too white room at the Health Center.

She has a two year old daughter already. Born in the heat of an early June. And as ridiculous as it may sound, she had always wanted two children. One girl. And one boy. A marriage with a faithful husband. The all American dream. Was there anything better? She sure didn't think so.

And the months and weeks and days went by faster than she remembered with her first pregnancy. Because all the sudden it was December. And the newborn would be coming anytime now. And everything has been going just as good as things should go for a young soon to be mother. But then again, there was one thing that even her physician couldn't help her with. Her dreams.

As time drew close for her baby son, her dreams began to suffer quite a bit. At first they were just dreams of a dark room. And at the entrance she would stand. She would not dare go in. She would just stand and listen to the sounds that came from the darkness. The sounds of a woman crying followed by the sound of a single baby. It cried as well. But as it would cry there was a gagging at the end of each sob. And right before she would awake in her bed and covered in sweat, there was always the sound of a deep and horrid growl. And as much as she did not want to admit it to herself, she knew that the growling came from her unborn son lost and crying from that darkened room.

This dream haunted her sleep for the first eleven days of that early month of December. And it just so happened that the night that her dreams decided to change was also the night before she would give birth to her son.

She had fallen asleep just after eleven that night while watching Johnny Carson with her husband next to her. He had passed out by then from a long days work and eight beers. Something that she herself couldn't wiat to do after she gave birth. She even had a six pack in the fridge waiting for her arrival from the hospital when she came home.

She dreamed of being in labor with her legs propped up and wide. Her husband was not in the delivery room, but her mother was. As well as the doctor and two nurses. And there was pain. A pain which seemed to have doubled within her this time around. And blood. So much blood.

"Get *it* out!" she screamed. "Oh please get... it ... OUT!"

"Just hold on. Stop shaking and hold on!" One of the nurses told her. There was fear in her face as well as the doctors. There hands and arms were covered in dark blood. It was almost black. And it was at this moment that she realized that this was no dream. It was all real. It was all really happening.

Her husband stood outside the room and next to the door. He wouldn't watch. But he sure was would be close enough to listen and hear his sons screaming voice. His nerves were shot. And he was sweating.

"What have we done?" he asked himself.

He held his hands together to keep them from shaking. It made him look as if her were praying. Some of the staff at the hospital looked, but paid no real mind. It was nothing new to see a grown man pray in a hospital. It was even one of those things that was at times advised.

Now he *did* pray.

"Dear Lord, forgive us for what we have done. Please take *it* away from us. This SIN. Please take it away. And forgive. Please forgive."

And it was at this moment that he heard his wife scream from inside the delivery room. His heart jumped. And he felt the hair on the back of his neck rise as chills ran over his back. He shivered and listened. There was a moment of silence and then he heard the sound of his son cry as well as the cry of his beloved wife.

Only she was not crying over the joy of becoming a mother again. She was crying for the horror that she knew she created.

She wanted him gone.

She *needed* him gone.

"Why?" She cried to her mother as she held her hand. "Why did I do this?"

Her son cried louder now. It was horrible for her parents to hear. And it made her cry harder.

"Oh God forgive me."

The crying. The blood. The screams of her new son.

"Forgive me."